WEST

WHITNEY POOLE

Underground Voices
Los Angeles, California
2015

Published by Underground Voices
www.undergroundvoices.com
Editor contact: Cetywa Powell

ISBN: 978-0-9904331-3-2

Printed in the United States of America.

WEST

1

Someone must have been telling lies to Sebastian Veillard. His father had not been arrested. It would have been easier if he had. What Sebastian could say was that his father had disappeared. That much was true. No current signs of the man remained in the house. The derelict building had exposed wires and missing floorboards. Sebastian had the feeling there was someone in the room, someone following him, but as he went from room to room he stood alone amid the decay of the house.

Ghosts of the past are hidden in the woodwork. That's what his father always said. By now Sebastian knew better. Houses don't have souls. There's nothing spiritual about them. Still they were his work. It's in the blood, his father would say. Now as he hammered his way through the old house, a flood of memories did not happen. There was only the one. His father broke a picture of his family and Sebastian left. Everything else had faded. Over time he had forgotten the details of his youth. Grain by grain the memories became dull. He felt numb all over just being in the house. It had been too long for him to feel anything real here again. The events of the past almost eluded Sebastian, but he felt them, dully, coming back. Sebastian's memory came back to him in waves. He had tried to forget. Almost everything had been erased. He moved on into a new city with a new life. Then the letter came.

The first few days Sebastian found his tools moved. He would leave them in one room and they would reappear in another. This and other occurrences made him think the house haunted. Stranger things have happened. In a house all but forgotten in the Old Quarter, this was a possibility. First the hammer disappeared from the entryway where Sebastian worked. He found it a few days later sticking out of a wall. The head had been pushed into the surface. The handle hung down from where it was lodged. Then his pliers disappeared. He couldn't do any work with the wiring without them. They reappeared attached to some live wires. He dislodged them with a broom.

These occurrences made him think there was someone else in the house, yet no matter how long he waited, he was the only one. That, too, eventually changed.

Upon returning Sebastian purchased wood to repair the house. His skills as a builder drove him, skills he learned from his father. The need to construct took control of him before he could sort through the mess his father left in the house. He knew something was wrong by the state of the place. His father wouldn't have left anything unfinished.

Something had happened, what he did not know. The city he left had found its way back into his life. He never wanted to come back. Too many painful memories lived here.

He felt the grain of the boards as he laid them down over the exposed beams. The edges were rough against his fingers. He imagined workmen paring trees down into lumber. Theirs was a life of division, of reduction, of making larger things smaller.

Sebastian eyed the stamp from the lumberyard as he aligned the board. Maybe the wood came from a factory. Trees were shoved through a machine, which sliced and separated the trunk at predetermined intervals. No piece was unique, just another piece resulting from efficient design.

He hammered a nail into the wood board. The report of the nail driving home echoed in the empty hall. Sebastian remembered fresh cut herbs placed in a vase in the hall. The place now smelled of dust. He aligned another board and hammered.

The heat was oppressive outside. He had shuttered all the windows he could to keep the inside of the house cool. Still, sweat rolled down his face as he hammered. A bead dropped on the floor.

Sebastian still could not directly face what had happened between him and his father. Even as he busied himself working on the house, he averted learning more about the mess his father left. The memories in the house were too strong.

Doors twice the height of an adult man had fallen off their hinges. The gaps in the doorframes connected the rooms of the house so that Sebastian could see from one end to the other without obstruction.

How could he have lived like this? he thought.

The sound of the hammer filled the house, echoing from the hallway into other empty rooms. Sebastian raised and lowered his arm hoping to control the memory that caused him to leave. There were so many things he would do different now, he thought.

He stopped to wipe sweat from his forehead and looked at his work on the floor. All the nails had been bent, driven crooked while he was thinking about his past.

He reached for more nails but felt someone was watching him. He had had this feeling before and found only the house; but this time was different. There was someone nearby who could reach out and touch him. Sebastian looked up from hammering floorboards and there stood Xavi, dressed neatly in an ecru linen suit, peering down at him through dust raised by hammer strokes.

Xavi Boleno. It had been a long time since Sebastian had heard that name. He remembered Xavi from his school days as an upright student who never strayed far from expectation. He had middling grades but always seemed to advance. Sebastian's father had opened his doors to Xavi when Xavi's parents died. He often came by to spend hours with Sebastian's family. The two had been close until Sebastian left the city. Since then, there wasn't a word until the letter.

"The door was open. I had heard you were back so I thought I should pay you a visit." Xavi's voice had a droll quality. He played with his words as he spoke them.

7

Sebastian stood, patting dust off his legs as he rose. "It's good to see you." He wiped beads of sweat from his brow with the back of his hand. The heat was more intense than he remembered.

Xavi strolled further in. With each step he evaluated the cornices and broken floorboards that remained in the house.

"Being here brings back some memories. You've really let this place fall apart."

"This is how I found it."

"Didn't believe it at first. There's no way you'd come back here, not after what happened between you and your father," Xavi said.

"Everyone knows about it? All these years I thought he'd bottle it up, let it drive him to extremes, just like everything else."

"It wasn't too difficult for anyone to piece together. You disappeared. Your father disappeared too, into his work."

"Well, there's not much left for me to disappoint now, except a threadbare house and warped boards. Why didn't you send for me earlier? I would have come if I had known. I need to know what happened."

Xavi turned toward Sebastian in the center of the entryway. "Send for you? I haven't thought about you in years."

"But the letter…"

"Someone's been playing tricks on you. I didn't send you a letter."

"You didn't?"

"Why would I do that? Things have been easy for me with you gone. Why would I ruin that?"

"But the letter…" Sebastian withdrew the note he received via his firm in Argentina.

Sebastian,

Your father disappeared a few weeks ago. I would have written sooner, but I wasn't sure what happened. No one was. We're not sure if he left or if he was abducted, maybe an accident somewhere far off in the city. I thought you should know.

Let's not let events from the past keep us apart. I know we've had our differences. There are reasons for all of us to be mad still after all these years. Don't let them keep you away. Things have changed for the worse too much.

I know relations between you two were strained. Especially since you left, I never thought you would come back. You have to now. There's no one to look after your father's building projects. He would want you here, for what it's worth. He and I became close while you were away. I know he never said any of it to you, but privately he told me he wanted your help. With what I'm not sure. That was part of the problem. No one knew what he was talking about anymore. It may not mean much, coming from him, but at least it's something

We heard about the Exhibition Center you built in Buenos Aires. It made him proud. He'd never say it but you could see the look in his eyes. He kept the magazine feature of the Exhibition Center on his desk for months. He never mentioned it but you knew it meant something to him.

Please come back. I hope this letter found you through your firm. We couldn't find any other way of contacting you, not even an e-mail address. Everything will fall apart if you don't.

-Xavi

Sebastian showed it to Xavi who skimmed it and tossed the sheet back to Sebastian.

"I didn't write that. Let's go for a drink. This is no place for a conversation. It's falling apart." With a pat on the shoulder, Xavi led the way out of Sebastian's house.

Xavi hadn't sent the letter. It arrived in the care of his architecture firm in Argentina. Apparently someone followed him close enough to know where he worked but not where he lived. But why would that person write a letter as Xavi? Sebastian did not know.

They walked through the plaça and along dark, angling streets. Occasional passersby could be seen walking along the cobbled stones underfoot. Night had fallen while Sebastian was at work restoring his family's house. People began to mill about in the cooler air of the evening. Sweat still clung to Sebastian's T-shirt. Xavi seemed at ease in his suit.

"Then my father ... is he still missing?"

"I'm afraid that part's true. No one has much of an idea what happened. He just disappeared one day."

At least the mystery of what happened to his father was true. The fact did not reassure him. Someone must have been waiting for the opportunity to bring him back. He did not like the thought of what he would find in the city. Already the place disturbed him. It had altered drastically since he left years ago.

"How did you know I came back?"

"My assistant told me. She has friends in customs. She keeps me apprised of anything that's worth knowing in this city. I should really pay her more."

Sebastian wondered at how Xavi was now acclimated to the city. He could not tell. He brushed dust off his jeans self-consciously and tried to let his senses become accustomed to night in the city. The sound of music echoed from ahead of them in the alley. Sebastian could see light filling an expanse of the plaça before them. The rest remained in darkness, hidden from the eyes of the city. Shadows of pedestrians grew long on the wall ahead of them. They moved like caricatures of real people, elongated and gesturing comically, as if conducting some ribald dance led by a puppeteer.

They entered the plaça in the light at the end of the narrow street. Tables lined the few restaurants around the plaça. In the center, was a raised stone platform, a few steps up, upon which some revelers had congregated. Empty bottles lined the steps. A few had been tipped sideways. They laughed and smiled at each other, their cheeks flush with alcohol under the heat. One man turned a woman as they danced. The couple laughed. The man dancing reached his arm around the woman's waist and drew her near. She giggled and lifted thick black hair above her head with arms inked with an intricate series of tattoos.

Another plucked a few strings on a guitar tentatively. Sebastian heard a bottle topple and roll. It thudded against the recess between the cobbled street and the raised platform. The man who knocked it over eyed Sebastian from his seat on the steps. He had a round, unshaven face with round bloodshot eyes. The man smoked slowly, inhaling his cigarette. Smoke rose to his pupils and stung the irises that followed Sebastian as he moved.

Xavi led the way through tables lined with white cloth to the entrance of one of the buildings on the plaça. Inside, cool air emanated from the marble in the entryway. A broad sloping staircase made of marble stood before them. Sebastian peered toward the roof as he crossed the entryway, twisting his head at the levels above him. They mounted the staircase, lazily spiraling upward. Its metal railing was ornately wrought beneath a smooth wooden banister.

"This city has changed."

"These streets look worse than they actually are," Xavi said.

At the landings, two tall pairs of wooden doors stood at each end. The solid frames were imposingly high. The doors were shut tightly leaving the two alone in a large, cavernous room through which they ascended.

The white marble floor cooled the air to a quiet still. Lamps lit the way up but they did not illuminate the entire space. Sebastian strained his eyes in search of steps at times.

"It's you that's really changed, my friend. If you had lived here, you could have seen the city change bit by bit. It hasn't been easy for anyone. Every day something new would happen. An old building goes down. A new one comes up. People breathe, have sex, have kids, get jobs, lose jobs, move, divorce. If you had stayed, you would have been surprised for a day then changed your idea of what seemed different. But you had to stay away. For you everything has changed all at once. That's the price you pay for leaving."

Sebastian forced a smile and shook his head. "I've got enough to handle without you lecturing me. Why would someone impersonate you in a letter to me? It doesn't make sense." Sebastian heard faint traces of people's voices. The darkness seemed to dissipate and light became more frequent again. On the fifth level, Xavi approached one of the pairs of wooden doors on the landing, seemingly at random, and rang an adjacent bell.

"You've got me. Anyone who wants to survive these days has to be flexible. Not too much, just enough so you don't break. There's all kinds of reasons. Not everyone can play the golden boy."

The dark cuts of wood hung heavily on the hinges. A worn nameplate arched forgotten above the entrance.

The door buzzed and they entered.

The two walked through a room with plush circular booths lining the walls. Smoke hung lazily in the air. They ordered cocktails from the bar that came in tall cylindrical glasses. Ice clinked against the sides of each glass as they walked out onto a terrace that overlooked the plaça below. Wisteria grew intertwined among the slats of a trellis running along the rooftop expanse. Women in light summer dresses and men in button down shirts chatted and laughed in small groups surrounding tall tables with low-backed metal chairs.

Sebastian forced a wry smile to his face. "Never could keep it straight, could you?"

Xavi eased back into his chair. "You've got to keep amused somehow."

"I never did."

"Sure, if you're telling it, you never asked for anything. Doubled the efforts anyone else would have put into it. I know that's bullshit. People have eyes. You did well because you were stubborn, and wouldn't submit to anyone, but above all because you had the luxury of opportunity. It's not like your father became who he was on his own, was it? He had it handed to him. Now look at you, resistant to the last, a decade's worth of wrinkles on your face and you still can't see it. Running away hasn't solved all that much. Finds you in the same circumstances, doesn't it?"

"You know that's not true. Don't tell me you came to see me only to laugh at my expense."

"Like I said, you've got to amuse yourself somehow."

"I rejected all that when I left. Can you tell me you got to where you are cleanly? You've no guilt eating at you at night?"

"You're mistaken in confusing sleep with night. Some of the best times of the day are found hidden in the hours before dawn."

The cries of the people dancing in the plaça rang out raucously. Their voices reverberated on the hard stone of the surrounding buildings and pealed up into the night air, where the sound would be lost amid the harsh sounds of traffic enveloping the outer regions of the city. From their stance on the terrace, Xavi and Sebastian were well removed from any of the cavorting below.

"The world will forget us the moment we turn around. Look at this place. No one here remembers anything. They forget the moment they go to bed. I may have wanted to leave all this behind, but I never forgot. No, the world is much more complex than these streets would have us think." Sebastian paused. "What happened here, Xavi?"

Xavi ordered another drink. "These streets? Just look at those two. That girl dancing below moves with life brimming in her veins. She lives more in a few steps than most do in their entire lives. We should be thankful we were fortunate enough to witness such passion." The shadows of the dancers grew tall on the walls of buildings below. The man with the round face had turned his gaze to the woman dancing.

"You're not answering me."

"You always were defiant, even cynical at times. It was your pride that got you into arguments in the first place." The alcohol took effect in his blood. Xavi slurred his words as he spoke. He finished his drink and asked for another.

"After all these years, you still can't tell me."

"What's to tell? No one here cares about your story. They've seen the same thing happen time after time. You're no different than anyone else. You don't have the right to waltz in and demand answers."

"You're right. You don't owe me. No one does anymore."

In the plaça below, the round-faced man tried to place his hands around the waist of the woman. The man dancing with her became angry and waved the other off. He shoved him and a fight broke out. Feet shuffled and the clatter of glass breaking echoed off the walls of the plaça.

The sound reached Xavi. A barely visible shiver ran through his body. He drained his glass and eyed the remaining ice mournfully. "Listen, your father didn't want to be part of this project any more than he wanted you to leave."

"And what would you know about that?"

14

"The man changed after you left. He really never stopped working. He took me under his guidance on a few projects. I remember going over plans with him well into the night and finding him at the site first thing in the morning. He even wore the same clothes, dusty as they were covered in debris."

"He was always like that."

"Not like this. I don't think he spent nights at the house. He lived where he worked. I think he was trying to erase something by plunging himself into whatever he was doing.

"With your father gone there are some opportunities opening up along various channels in the city. A man with ambition could get somewhere. Remember Grey? He doles out all the city contracts. He handled all the contracts your father worked on. The two worked closely on this from the start. If you want to know what he was working on, talk to Grey. It could help your career on this side of the ocean as well."

"I'll look into it. Where can I find him?"

"He's in the Ministry of Development now. His projects are all over the city."

"Where's the project my father was working on?"

Xavi laughed. "You still haven't seen it? It's been right in front of you all this time. Just look and you'll find it." He rose to leave. He had swayed a bit as he turned to take in the scene behind him on the terrace.

"Just tell me where it is."

"That would take all the fun out of it. Imagine, you in your own city without a clue where to go. I'll leave you to it, Sebastian. God knows you have some catching up to do." Xavi patted him on the back and left.

Sebastian thought back to his father's writings and called after Xavi. "You don't know what *West* means, do you?"

He spoke over his shoulder with a wave of the hand, "No more than anyone else," and lost himself at the bar.

2

He had returned too late to see his father. The man had vanished, leaving only stillness to greet Sebastian Veillard. It's been too long since I've been here, he thought. Through distance, age obscures. Memories of his childhood were slow to come. The place was threadbare now. Most of the valuables in the house had been sold. Only dusty outlines of wealth remained. Sebastian peered out the window into a sun that shined indifferently on each passing day. His past was present only as a lament from the city that swept through the cooling streets of the neighborhood at dusk. During the day, no one cared. Any connections with the city had faded while he was abroad. They would not return any time soon. In the stillness, Sebastian dwelt seeking for the phantom knowledge of his dead father.

The windows, where they weren't broken, were smudged with a thick layer of grime. Sebastian dipped a sponge into soapy water. The suds were absorbed into the pores of the sponge. Sebastian splashed water onto the base of the sill as he washed the windows. The effect was not prodigious. Instead of cleaning the glass, the dust smeared into large streaks. With every pass of the sponge he was moving the dust around. He tried renewing the water but the bucket was already dark with grime.

Sebastian looked through the hole in one window and saw a checkered mess of red tiles. So many were broken that the roof looked more white than red. He could see people passing on the street from here.

The wind blew in from an open door overlooking the garden. The air was stirring outside and began to lift through the hallways of the Veillard house. The scent of the sea crept lazily through the darkness. The heat of the sun was beginning to burn in the air outside. He had been gone too long. The house he inherited was a faint whisper of the home he had once known. The light fixtures were broken in most of the halls. Spidery wires twirled from the walls like the gnarled tendrils of a diseased tree. From his candlelight he saw the floorboards were missing ahead. Only a few wooden planks crossed the rafters. He balanced across them peering through the darkness below into what should be the entryway. Walking onto the veranda overlooking the garden, he listened to the movement of the sea. Sound rushed in from the sea, weaving across and through the streets leading up to the hills.

Sebastian descended a long, sloping staircase toward the entrance. The scent of the garden trickled in from the courtyard adjacent to the entranceway. The Iberian flora carried a richness that grew from more than the soil housing it. Its peculiar aroma had been cultivated over centuries. Even now with the house in disrepair, the vegetation was pushing forth from the earth to flourish. Sebastian took one last look at his house and pushed open the large wooden door to the street outside.

Steps fanned out from the pair of wooden slabs that sequestered his home from the scene outside. A small street that ran perpendicular to him led in and away from the square on the far side. Little traffic came through this thoroughfare. Two separate side streets emptied in to the square as well; one ran along the side of his house to the right, the other ended across the square slightly askew from his home's entrance. These cut through the web of winding alleys that comprised the old quarter of the city. So small in their breadth, only a few people could walk through them at a time. They were useful when navigating the Old Quarter on foot, but Sebastian began to notice that they had fallen into misuse. Trash lined their edges. It had even begun to spill forth into the square in front of his house. Even the few shops in the square seemed more haggard than before. Where a small market had sold its wares to the local residents, a shuttered shop hid its face from the public. These and other curiosities were beginning to vex Sebastian. He had time until his meeting was to start. He set out to cross the square and visit the vendor who lived in the corner of the square corner when his path was obstructed.

A car pulled into the square from a street perpendicular to his path. It was a black vintage sedan that appeared to have been waiting for him. One of the shining windows rolled down and a head shot out, "Grey sent us for you."

On its hood a silvery pair of wings flew backward in ornamentation. The street was empty. It was tucked away from most of the streets comprising the tangled web of the barri. The din of the gathering mass was quieted by the high rising walls. A man was holding the door open for Sebastian at the rear of the car. He sat and waited as his escorts drove him through the city.

The car rumbled regularly as it rode on the cobbled streets leading away from the Veillard house. The streets had been designed in a different age. Sebastian noted that the car barely fit between the encroaching walls of the surrounding buildings. He stared blankly out the windows into the stony, textured wall mere inches beyond the glass. Tall, rectangular windows with shutters wide open stared back at him intermittently. Their vigil was dark under the dawning light. It could not yet reach these valleys carved between the ramble of buildings. The car turned onto a broader avenue leading away from the warren that was Sebastian's home - the Old Quarter.

Street signs began to appear at regular intervals. Less people crowded the streets and they quickly drove through the staccato procession of lights. After a few minutes, they rode along an expansive route leading away from the sea into the newer quarters of the city.

The city has grown, Sebastian thought as he looked off to the edge of the city. It crept upon the verdant slopes. Along the horizon, the wind dissipated into the royal hues of the setting sun. Those mounds of raised earth encircled the city enclosing it into a world all its own. The sea's roving roared as a constant in the world Sebastian remembered.

Neither of his escorts spoke. Sebastian weighed them with his eyes. The driver was a solidly set man. His shoulders were square in the confines of the car. He hardly moved, save to turn the wheel, and wore a black suit, which added to his overall motionless character. His eyes were covered by a pair of sunglasses that hid his intent. The other, the one who had called him, was identical in every respect except for the sunglasses. This one had the habit of staring and leaning in as he spoke. His tone seemed one recorded by another and played by this enactor on cue. Their frames were well built and brimmed beyond the confines of the seats. Such sentinels would be imposing figures should he ever encounter them on the streets alone. He was glad for their stolid escort for the moment.

Sebastian's gaze turned to the city that was passing by him as he rode. Later he corrected this notion and saw that it was he who was passing by the city, not it by him. He marveled at how it had changed in his absence. He tried to mend the surface of those whirring streets with his memory. They had become so elusive in his distance from the place. He did not think that physical separation could ruin the very essence of a place in one's mind. It was a notion ill conceived. He had hoped that the sites of the city would evoke more memories but found only a shiny new world encircling him. As a boy he knew the towns that now merged into this one rambling city. The new buildings of the Expansion had arisen seemingly out of nowhere. Its orderly blocks and high-rising building were an aberration against the organic development of the older quarter. He contemplated the convivial days of his youth as he let himself be chauffeured through the presently airy and straight avenues. Even abroad, in more developed lands, such modern conveniences were luxuries rather than commonplaces. He delved deeply for the semblance of recognition in this stretch of land he had known so long; but he found his thoughts lacking.

The car rolled up out of the Expansion into a winding route along the hills that were verdant in the distance from his house. The wheels were spinning smoothly over the meandering curves of the road that led up from the city. The car began to snake back and forth languidly as it ascended. Their destination was near.

Sebastian peered down on the city as it unfolded. It looked foreign from here. All of the splendor, sweat, and tears of artisans' hands was unnoticeable on the buildings from this distance. The buildings blended into one another as a contiguous mass of materials. Beyond was the sea, but its waves were diminutive through the haze of distance.

The car slowed to a crawl as they reached the gate of a building nestled securely amid the folds of hills. High walls fenced in the structure within. They were of a cream color with reddish brown tiles crowning the top. A large, forbidding steel gate gave way for them and they entered.

Sebastian noted a garden, which spread from behind the central structure off to the shallow side of the hill. It was neatly trimmed and terraced into several levels. Pathways formed an intricate network leading through the vegetation. They were sparse enough to provide privacy between them.

They parked in front of the central structure. It appeared to be a house, but within high steep walls. Windows were regular and tiered upon its face. A thick stone fence encircled the elevated building. The fence was raised upon a hill so that when Sebastian approached, it stood twice his height. Off to his right, away from the garden, the exterior wall ran close to the house. It adorned the crest of a hill with the upper levels of the house rising above it. Those windows had a commanding view that impressed Sebastian with the likeness of a fortress.

After the rise in his surroundings, the upper levels piled upon one another securely. Each was slightly narrower than the next, and Sebastian felt they were askew to produce views in all directions throughout the house. Minarets rose from the corners emphasizing its height as it reached toward the heavens from the hills.

He entered through the doors that were being held open for him alone. He left his escorts behind.

There were supplicants in high backed chairs lining the walls of the antechamber. Sebastian studied their faces as he was ushered past their rows. Each had the sullen look of one continually waiting to be called, but left ever expecting. The supplicants wore pernicious suits that seemed to close too tightly at the neck. Perhaps this was the reason for their rigid posture. Sebastian paid them little mind as their heads turned to follow the man being granted access while they waited. He was glad for his departure from their hungry, obedient looks when he entered Grey's office.

At the back of the room, a tall well-groomed man stood behind a large desk. He was flipping through the pages of some kind of ledger. His finger traced the information he was looking for and closed it. Sebastian greeted him diffidently.

"It hasn't been so long now, has it?" Grey reflected.

The man walked from behind his desk. He shook Sebastian's hand firmly and patted his shoulder. The two sat. "It seems just the other day when your father and I were meeting just like this. I was sorry to hear of his disappearance. One does what one can to survive in today's world. Your father knew that quite well. Have you seen much of the city since you've been back?"

"Only the house."

"I know it must be quite a shock. Things have changed, Sebastian. I remember some of the works your father did in this city. They were proud endeavors." He stopped for a moment and wistfully stared off into the hills beyond his home. A pang of regret welled in Sebastian.

"Do you know what happened?"

"At the time, he was working on a trade center. There was a lot of interest from the city in having a new, more modern place for business. There are opportunities out there for everyone these days. Several investors, including myself, approached him. He had taken the endeavor on and was well into construction when it happened. It was going to be something unique, I tell you." Grey waxed wistfully at his own words, dreaming of what would have been before he added as an anecdote, "We're working on finishing it as we speak."

He continued. "He was a master, one of the true citizens of the city. He changed the face of the city in our lives. But what can one do? One day he was supervising the trade center, the next he never returned. Construction stopped. It was all his idea, you see. He had everything planned out but never shared any of it. No one had any idea what to do. He sequestered himself in the house. We implored him to return but there was no response. Imagine that, a man like your father barring himself from the world! It took some time to decide what to do. Expenses were growing by the day. By the time we resolved to resume the project, no one had seen him for months. Someone returned to inform him and found the house open. It was completely empty. The house had been gutted, and most of its holdings had been pawned off, or so we presume."

"But why? I can't understand how this could have happened."

"I'm not quite sure either, Sebastian. It's been months since he's been gone and no one's been able to turn anything over. We tried to track him down, of course. When we went in, we saw the state of affairs the house was in. There was no trace of anything. I suppose word took so long to reach you because we were holding out hope for him to just reappear, just as he vanished. There was nothing left, you see? A shame you only now just heard."

Sebastian was growing stern thinking of the state of his decrepit house. His predecessor was a man who had taken his word solemnly. He was a man of integrity. He would not have abandoned any of his work, much less the city he loved. It was hard for Sebastian to begrudge the fact that his father had abandoned everything that defined him.

Grey went on. "I know, son. It's hard. But, dead or not, he's gone. That's something we've all had to accept."

Sebastian was becoming irritated with his helplessness in the situation. It was frustration that defined him as the sun's rays intruded from the windows behind Grey. The burden stretched taut in the air of the room. His seizing confusion would have stifled any speech Sebastian had left if Grey had not continued on, ignoring Sebastian's demeanor.

"Come, let's go for a walk outside."

The two adjourned to the dawning light so majestic on the hills. The temperature was rising in a rush of august and beleaguered heat. Grey's frame carried with it a firm grace. He stood forward, raising his head to survey the surrounding land. "You're a man who's a longstanding member of the tradition of this little city. But I think it's evident to everyone that this is no longer such a little city. It teems, my friend. It teems with opportunity." Grey's words came to a close slowly as Sebastian weighed them in his head. "To most ordinary men, men of no breeding or couth, this lost inheritance would be crippling, but you, you're a man of a different sort. You have the poise to change your destiny. And, seeing as how our families have been so long acquainted with each other, I've elected to give you that opportunity."

"What opportunity?" The words came dryly from his lips.

"I want you to be a part of this. Resume your father's work."

Sebastian hated the man for his importunity. He had no sense of loss. The last remark drew to mind the missing tiles on his roof. The checkered mess reminded him of the sparseness of his house. It was an eerie twilight where his thoughts dwelt. He remembered the empty rooms of his house where his family had dwelt. They were no more. It was out of this labyrinth that he felt compelled to escape.

"No. It was his work, not mine."

"We saw the work you did in Buenos Aires. Quite impressive."

"I needed to create something of my own."

"That's just the kind of vision we need. Your father's work, it was respectable but his last few months didn't meet expectations. I think you should think over what has been said here. I'll lend you some money in the interim while you re-acclimate yourself to the climate here. It's been a long time, Sebastian."

"That's not necessary."

Grey was ushering him out the door as he spoke. His meeting was apparently at an end. "Come by and let me know how things are progressing. I could use a man like you these days. It's hard to find men of character." The door closed behind him and Sebastian stood looking at the fat envelope Grey had placed in his hands. He was in the anteroom with all the other onlookers waiting for their audiences. He felt disgusted by their eager, wagging faces and left as quickly as he could.

The stairs descending from the villa seemed to be endless. Sebastian managed them in an irksome mood. The meeting had proved distasteful. He was beginning to feel the day being curdled by it when he looked to the sky. The sun was passing over the hills spreading its august colors. It reminded him of impermanence. Yet the fiery orb would come again. It always did.

A thin mane in a neat suit waited for him next to a car at the bottom of the steps with the same two escorts. The man wore wire glasses that caught the glint of sunlight. His short, styled hair parted to one side.

"My name is Arturo. I'm an aide to the minister."

"I've already met with him."

"He asked me to meet with you before you left. Things aren't finished as they stand. We need someone to come on board who can clean things up. Tie up all the loose ends of projects, if you will."

"That's not why I'm here."

"You've a track record. The minister knows about the exhibition center you built. You built it in less than a year. He's impressed. We need that kind of perseverance."

"There are other things on my mind right now."

"Come see him at his offices tomorrow. Don't worry about how things ended. He wants to see you. Here's the address. We can talk about how the minister wants you involved in affairs."

"I never said I wanted to take on any new projects. I've got enough work back home."

"Don't be silly. The opportunities you have here are on a far larger scale than anything you're used to. Only an idiot would pass up the chance."

Sebastian took the card and entered the car.

"I almost forgot. You're looking for your father, aren't you? There was a piece of writing, Borges' work, he was fond of — *The Aleph*. An aleph is a portal through which you can see all other points, a kind of visionary symbol. I heard your father carried a copy of the story around with him. He studied it like a bible. He was convinced an aleph existed in the city. It's a point through which you can see all other points. I have a copy of the story for you. It might help you in your search. I've found it an interesting read. I don't think your father found any alephs though."

The escorts closed the door. Their forms were dark, imposing silhouettes upon the horizon as the car disappeared down the sloping, winding path that led towards the crossed streets of the city.

3

Sebastian looked drearily upon the buildings whose reflections shone on his face in the car's window. Their high shining faces stared blankly at him. It was all so strange, the city and the bills in his pocket. He felt so far from the Veillard he thought himself to be. He caught himself wondering at the sound of his own name. It lolled hard in his throat as he practiced it silently in the car.

He imagined the sunset in the hollow eyes of the buildings. Later, white lights would appear, one by one, as if a new star was being born every moment. He would be awash in a sea of dazzling lights that erased the memory of those hideous buildings. No love was crafted in their artifices. Such passion was left to artists.

An aleph. In Borges' story the aleph is about two centimeters in length. It exists in someone's basement. Once you see the aleph, you can see everywhere through it. It's a point that contains all other points. Arturo said Sebastian's father was searching for it. Sebastian didn't believe they existed.

The many faces of a crowd parted around the car. The car was heading from the broad avenues of the Expansion, where glossy buildings rose, orderly as towers above the ambling confines of the Old Quarter. His gaze caught hold of something recognizable in the blur of images. He ordered his driver to stop and stepped out of the car into the heavy light of midday.

"I want to walk from here."

"Suit yourself."

Sebastian wended his way back toward his house, picking his way between the streets of the Old Quarter, trying to remember what the city looked like when he had left so many years ago.

Large department stores and shiny shop windows were illuminated by the afternoon sun. The shimmering glass dazzled patrons walking past. Sebastian brushed past them. These faceless bodies drifted among the crowds from shop to shop. Along their floating path, pale apparitions greeted their wants as they pointed and salivated in the street. Their satiation was of a trivial sort. Sebastian glanced at one last group as he left the square. Translucent smiles displayed on panes. Their bodies were opaquely visible in the reflection upon the glass. The two sets of apparitions frightened his very sense of self with their anonymity, for he knew at every shop window, there was a pair.

Darkness began to fall. It crept slowly up from the corner of the street. As the sun went further west, the height of buildings cast a shadow encompassed by the network of streets in the Old Quarter. The gothic walls turned first to a rich golden hue before being covered in shadow. Hours before sunset, you could only see the sun at the top of tall buildings, scintillating off windows while the neighborhood below fell to night. The nocturnal appetites of the city began to grow. Business workers hurried home, their pressed shirts and briefcases crisp in the darkening air. Housewives opened the shutters to their houses. The smell of dinner cooking accosted the unwary traveler in pockets of aroma that collected in the nooks where wind ceased to travel. Children kicked soccer balls in the street, running heartily without a real knowledge of exhaustion. Those who slept during the afternoon would rise soon and meander out into the streets from couches or beds of grass in city parks. Their nights just beginning, their appetites just wetted, they would create the spark of electricity that hummed with the night.

It was this energy through which Sebastian now walked.

He looked at the restaurants and tapas bars brimming with the passions that were nursed during the day. Their incubation complete, they emerged from the chrysalis of sleep to flit about the night air like gnats hungry for sustenance in their waking moments. The sound of chatter, of the ice in drinks melting, of plates clattering as they were swept away, of music, of dancing, of streetlights buzzing filled him with a beautiful cacophony of the livable, audible experience of life. He felt at once invigorated and frightened, for he knew it would not last.

Eventually people would tire. The vibrancy of this world would be replaced by one of weariness. The lights would blur before going out completely. The cafes and bars would empty. The streets would become an empty space, a warren of neglect, through which Sebastian would wander alone.

Thoughts of why he left came to him as he traveled through streets that should have been familiar to him but were not any longer.

*

All the guests had left.

Grief swept over him in waves that stung of nettles. He felt paralyzed in the high backed chair of the living room. Rigid and upright, they all dressed formally for the occasion. His tie choked the throat. He wrestled the knot out and away from him. Their silence was maddening to Sebastian.

The scene after the funeral bore a palpable brittleness. Sebastian knew how much his mother worked at mending the loose threads between people. She would place flowers centrally throughout the house and open curtains so that the sun streaked in, glinting off glass vases, and caught the eyes of anyone who had fallen sullenly into introspection. She never would stand for that kind of morose existential dread. Julía and she took to working on flower arrangements most Sundays. They took gardenias, tied them together or placed them delicately with their stems juxtaposed artfully.

Xavi sat rigidly on one of the leather couches that crinkled under the weight. Someone had hand sewn the bolts of material so that they fit around the frame with an upholsterer's touch. His black suit and tie drained all the pallor from his skin and beads of sweat bolted down the sides of his temples, along the crevasses next to his nose, and along the corners of his lips, down his chin. The boy's father died before he could form memories. Sebastian's father brought him into their home often because of his friendship with the man. This experience was probably Xavi's first encounter with grief. He stared off vacantly watching as the old man rearranged things above the fireplace.

"Why didn't she say anything?" Xavi asked.

"Some things are private," the father added.

The old man adjusted picture frames and vases on the mantle, inching a piece in one direction then rotating another into place.

"She knew she would die and she told us nothing. Why would she do that to us?"

"Say something. Anyone."

Julia's sobs filled the room as the silence returned. Veillard scraped a vase on the wood and as he drew the picture of his wife close.

"I told her not to."

"What?"

"No."

"Why would you do such a thing as that?"

"No one could know."

Sebastian rose. He attempted to stare straight at his father as he spoke. "You're irrational. I don't think you know what you're saying anymore. That doesn't make any sense." Sebastian approached his father and faced him. He grabbed his father's collar with both hands and shook, "Can't you feel anything? Can't you see you drove her to this? I blame you."

Glass shattered. His father clenched the picture so hard that the glass broke. His fingers poked through the photo, crumpling it and the shattered splinters of the frame in a bloody fist. "You don't know anything." Veillard's features remained unmoved.

Sebastian looked to Julía who stood open faced and teary. "At least you can cry."

Without his mother, there was no one to hold the family together. Scenes like this did not occur when she was alive.

The old man turned from the fireplace to look at his son for the first time since his mother died. "She knew. She knew what she was doing. That was her way of saying goodbye."

Sebastian felt the urge to hit him. He channeled the energy down toward his feet, pressed his toes firmly against the floorboards, and turned on them. He walked steadily from the room. Julía looked up from her abashed crying on the couch where she and Sebastian's mother used to arrange flowers. Her eyes opened unbelievingly as she sniffled. She stood and ran after him as he made his way down the hallway, leaving them all behind, running down the stairs. She implored him as he reached the door to stop. They needed him.

He thought about how he called his mother from across the street. He thought about the dog she stopped to scratch behind the ears, how he followed her into the street loyally as she crossed, the people queued up waiting for the bus, the smell of bread baking nearby, birds chirping at a nearby shop. He waved and she smiled, crossing the street, arms full of bags, with the dog following. It trotted beside her; and as she looked down to admire her new companion, she looked away from the bus that pulled into her.

Over her body, lying inert on the street while blood spilled out from her head, he heard the chirping constantly, callous cries unleashed into the air. The dog licked her head as Sebastian fell to the ground next to her, sobbing and touching her face as if he could still speak to her, as if she could still listen.

The memory faded. "No one here needs me."

West

On that day, Sebastian left.

4

West. The word was everywhere. Sebastian read it on the walls of the house. Big dripping letters reached up toward the ceilings from the floor where he walked.

At the other end of the hallway was his father's study. Sebastian drew up the courage to venture inside. There was too much that was unknown about what had happened to his father. No matter how difficult it would be, he had to look.

He approached the door, the floorboards creaking as he went slowly. His fingers grasped the worn metal knob. It jiggled at his touch. He strengthened his grip and turned. The door was locked. Locked? he thought. How could it be locked? No one lived here. There was no keyhole either. He pushed firmly on the door, then wrenched his wrist against the knob trying to break it. The door did not give. He butted his shoulder into the wood several times, grunting as he made impact until the door gave way and he found himself in his father's study.

It was one of the few rooms in the house that looked as if it were inhabitable. Sebastian felt drawn to it now. He entered the study and picked up a journal from the desk. A path of dust cleared on the surface as he drew the book to him.

Sunlight was breaking into the shade of the house with bolts that spread flatly upon the floor through tall windows. They were broad, merciless rays. The book in which his father's words were written had collected a commendable layer of dust. The spidery scrawl danced about the page without reason. He thumbed through the ragged pages of the derelict book as the sole inheritor of an empty estate. Its yellowed parchment was nicked and worn with age. Page after page rambled cryptically about whatever crossed the path of the old man's scribbling. Sebastian read the characters with the wrenching realization: his father had been mad. His eyes traced the scrawl, not recognizing the erratic lettering tapering as that of his father. The man was more direct, more controlled than this, Sebastian thought.

And still, even more bizarre: the former Veillard had written over the previous entries. Some pages were covered completely in what looked to be invented characters to him, but from what language he could not tell. Others were adorned with symbols and drawings of all sorts. The only part he understood was repetition of the word "west" everywhere.

He was afraid of what he might learn about the man. These pages were direct conduits into the man's thoughts. The scribbles were mad, and the old man had devoted his last days to it. They were self-indulgent ones, spent doting on age's eccentricities.

Sebastian read one of the more coherent passages.

They are all going missing, every one of them. I couldn't trust them before they disappeared, but now that they are gone I have nothing but doubts. Did they really work for me? I cannot be sure. Even now as I think back on them I have no assurances that they actually existed. Take the man I met on the street the other day. I stumbled upon him by chance, almost knocking him over in my preoccupation with work. He dusted himself off and retrieved his valise from the street. I was about to apologize when I recognized him. It was our foreman. He had disappeared so suddenly. No one knew what he had been doing. There was only an absence in our workings where he should have been. I barraged him with a flurry of questions about where he had been and why he hadn't finished his work. He looked at me nonplussed. As if it were me who didn't exist. How could any man have such an effect? How could any one person create such chaos in the order of things? He stared at me as if I were the madman and walked away in haste.

He and the others could not have been who they said they were. None of them. It was impossible. When I asked the foreman about it days after the incident, he had no recollection then as well. They are conspiring in this together. All of them.

And later, the old man had written over the passage in his spidery scrawl.

West. HE DID IT. It was him! All along it was him! Trust no one. They're in it together.

The passage went on but it was difficult to maintain the man's line of reasoning with all the scribbling and words scratched out in the text. The man truly had gone mad. It was difficult for Sebastian to come to terms with this fact. Anytime one's relative loses his faculties, it is difficult, but to see it happen before his eyes was too much for Sebastian.

Still, he thought, I must persevere. I must not flinch. He knew his father wouldn't, but perhaps this was the reason he went mad.

This house, this house is engulfing me. Every inch reminds me of something lost, something I've sacrificed over the last few years, and for which I have nothing to show. It's damning me to this existence, one I should have relented to a long time ago, but I continue. I can't stop. There is something inside of me, consuming me as I walk down these empty halls, thinking of how many other houses are the same, how many fathers walk through empty houses, sacrificing whatever they have left. I walk and mourn for those lonely souls, knowing that as each day passes I become more like the ghosts of these men who go through life without any purpose. Everything that mattered to them has gone. All that remains is a lament, one that is slowly being forgotten. I can hear their howls at night. Somewhere below the din of life that happens in cafes and restaurants during the night, somewhere below the clamor of dance clubs and cars roaring through the streets, I hear their low, piercing moan. It is full of sadness and pain. In it I hear their lumbering steps measuring the loss they have taken. Eventually, they forget the loss. Only the sensation remains. They forget how they came to the state they are in, forever cursed to walk through the streets of the city without anyone to recognize them, not even themselves. I cringe at such a fate, but already I see it looming.

What had he been trying to say, he thought. There was Xavi, the house, his father, Grey — they all were phantoms in his life. Together they should constitute some answer to the strange world he now inhabited. Sebastian knew he should be able to piece it all together. It was clear to him earlier, but these phantoms remained phantoms, obscuring his past, one that was quickly evaporating in the prevailing winds.

Sebastian read further.

He must be the replacement, the skinny one. There's no one else. I wish it weren't him. I wish there were others to choose from. He skims the surface of things, not like my boy. My boy knew how to work. He could see to the core of things. Now he's gone. Left me. I can't think of him anymore. It does me no good. I spend my days in the study wondering at how he left. How could he do this? What has happened to him, my boy? I hoped that he would take everything up. He could do it, I know. But the replacement, Xavi, he'll have to work. He doesn't have the talent. Not like my boy. Grey says he wants someone to know what I'm doing, just in case something happens. There needs to be a backup, a blueprint, for others to follow. Put it down for us. 'Us.' Who did he mean by us? I was not included in that 'us.' I'll not put anything down. It will stay in my head. All anyone will have are these words and they'll do no one any good. It takes a living person to do my work. If the replacement won't do it, no one will. He'll have to figure it out on his own.

Sebastian wondered at Xavi being the 'skinny one.' He had trouble believing the words he read. He and his father had never been close. Their relationship was contentious. Sebastian doubted the man saw any worth in him. Everything he did provoked a condemnation of some sort.

Sebastian closed the book and pushed it aside. No matter how much he wanted to learn, it was difficult to see a man unravel before your eyes. Sadness at everything he had lost, everything he had tried to forget, by being away for the last few years welled within him, but all he could do was laugh. He laughed and the sound of his laughter filled the empty, decrepit house that he once called his home.

He returned to the far end of the hallway.

He grasped the smooth, wooden handle of the hammer and began to work. He swung steadily, without any real purpose in mind other than to replace the echoes of haunting laughter that ran along the walls overhead with the sound of something he could control.

The old wooden beams splintered as Sebastian was prying them loose. Sebastian cut himself on a jagged end. He swore to himself, and wished everything weren't in ruin. He was beginning to realize it would be nearly impossible to rehabilitate the house, but he could not leave it untouched. As long as he lived, he would have to work on it, to restore the house to something resembling the living.

*

What was he working on? Grey hadn't been clear of the project though he certainly wanted Sebastian in the fold with him. There was so much Sebastian did not understand — the streets of the city, Xavi's indifference, Grey's newfound importance.

He decided to visit the Ministry of Development to see what kinds of projects his father had been involved with. So much of the journal talked about Grey, about what he was doing to the city. There was no way around him. Whether Sebastian liked it or not, he had to go further into the tangled mess of projects Grey must deal with. It was not a prospect Sebastian looked forward to, but if he were to find anything out about his father Grey had to help him.

5

The Ministry of Development's office was situated in a long row of new buildings. They were all shiny glass and boxed frames. Sebastian could smell the sea somewhere nearby but the view was obscured by the emerging business district. He craned his neck to look up the façade of the Ministry. From further up, he would see the water, but from where he stood on the street Sebastian could only imagine the waves.

Sebastian entered into a marble atrium full with lush plants that weren't native to the region. The sounds of a tranquil pool reached his ears as he checked in with the front desk. He pushed a button and waited for the elevator to take him to the twelfth floor. In between the doors, he noticed a pond filled with orange koi, some idly swimming, others darting after bits of food. He wondered at how Grey had landed so comfortably as he rode the elevator.

Sebastian emerged into a long reception area. There was a line of supplicants sitting on high backed chairs on either side of the wall. This was a strange practice of business that had developed in his absence. Sebastian stepped between the opposing lines of visitors, who seemed rather perturbed at Sebastian's boldness to talk to the receptionist waiting at the end of room.

She weighed him with her eyes as he approached, which took quite a bit longer than he expected with everyone watching him as he passed.

"I'm here to see the minister."

"And who are you?"

"I'm Sebastian Veillard."

She eyed him dubiously then began furiously jabbing at the keys of her computer. Her fingers moved so quickly that the symphony of her keystrokes filled the otherwise awkward silence of the room. A man to

Sebastian's left clutched his briefcase more closely to his lap. On the other side, a few men shuffled their feet anxiously.

The symphony stopped. The receptionist stared at the screen thoughtfully. "Here you are. The minister is scheduled to meet you, well, now. I'm afraid he's not in at the moment though." She addressed Sebastian directly with this last bit, as if it were the end of the matter.

"Do you know when he might be back?"

"Let me see." Again, the furious keystrokes filled the room. Sebastian waited a moment for the answer. "No, I can't say. He should have been here early this morning, and for that matter, he should have been here earlier this week, but no one has heard from him to date."

"I'm doing him a favor by being here."

"Doing him a favor? That's not the way it works. I'm sorry he's not in. You can have a seat if you like."

Sebastian turned to face the lines of supplicants. Their eyes were sad, with both hunger and humility combating for dominance. One clenched and unclenched his hat nervously. Another had slumped in his chair, gazing forlornly at the carpet. An upright man read and reread documents while murmuring his introductions.

Sebastian wondered if he would ever find the truth without seeing what his father worked on. That seemed central to the mystery. "Tell him that I'd like to pick up where we left off." Sebastian retraced his steps through the line of supplicants and took the elevator down.

On the way out of the elevator, as he passed through the lobby toward the street, someone called his name. The lobby appeared empty, save for a few office workers in the atrium, leather chairs, a few planted trees, glass windows facing the street, a dozing security guard, and a lone woman whose beguiling eyes weighed him with hurt pride and wonder.

Julía was not the only woman he had loved, but she was the one Sebastian remembered when love came to mind. All that was lost when he left. He did not even say goodbye, wishing to save her the grief of choosing between him and her life in the city.

She arched an eyebrow and asked, "You've finally come back?"

"I owe you an apology."

"Apology? The time for that has passed."

"My father's gone."

"You know, you could have called. It's not everyday that someone vanishes. You were like a ghost. No one knew what happened to you. Now, no one cares."

The receptionist tilted his head up from the desk in the lobby. He was beginning to take an interest in their conversation.

"Can we talk about this someplace else?"

"What are you doing here?"

"I had a meeting with Grey."

"You got an appointment?"

"He wasn't there, but we met yesterday."

"You actually met him? Consider yourself lucky. I've been trying to meet with him for weeks. They keep directing me to other departments."

The receptionist interjected. "Miss, the minister is not someone who can help you. He has much more official business to attend to."

"Why do you want to meet with him?"

"I need someone to open some doors for me. People tell me he's the person to talk to if you want anything done."

"That's not what he does, miss. Please be calm. You need to file a report with the police."

"I already filed a report with the police, you ass. They won't do anything until I get an official to make it a priority case. That's what Grey can do."

"I don't make the rules, miss."

"But Grey works development," Sebastian interjected.

"All the same, the paths keep leading here. They won't even let me up to his level. Assholes. Let's get out of here. I've had enough of being pushed around." She shoved a stack of neatly ordered papers off the desk toward the receptionist and walked out.

*

Julía and Sebastian left the office and ambled toward the sea in silence. With each step, they drew closer to the rhythm they once had, but from far apart now, as if crossing continents to perform a forgotten waltz.

They passed bageutinas, flower stands, tobacco shops, and newspaper kiosks. The florid aroma of the passing shops reminded them both of memories running through the streets.

"I can't believe them. It's so frustrating. No one in this city is willing to help. They're all too concerned with covering their own asses."

"What do you need help with?"

"I'm looking for my daughter."

"You have a child?"

"Enough. I can't talk about it anymore. It's too aggravating. What happened to you? You took off years ago and I run into you by accident? You've got some explaining to do."

Sebastian was withdrawn, uncertain of how to begin. He thought of all the things he could have said when he last saw her. He thought of why he left, of why he said nothing that night, when they sat on a bench along the port, huddled close as they watched a canopy of stars ripple when waves washed in one after another, but ultimately, he knew he had been selfish. He had cared too much about getting away and not enough about who he had hurt in his escape.

Julía's heels clacked against the sidewalk. The sound echoed against the surrounding shops leading down the street toward the port. A lazy dog pricked up his ears from where he lay at the foot of a magazine stand as she passed, her chin held high, eyebrow arched, expectant of an answer, unwilling to let Sebastian go unpunished.

A cacophony of calls sang out from caged birds for sale on the street. An old man read the paper, oblivious to the noise. Smoke wrinkled his face and he shuffled the pages before looking up at Julía. Her eyes had always beguiled Sebastian.

Cool, briny air felt damp on Sebastian's cheeks. A large expanse of stonework extended inland from the quay where boats were moored. Round white tables dotted the landscape. They were lightweight and easily portable for the waiters who carried them into the surrounding restaurants at night. Waves rushed onto the sand further down the shore, dragging with each unfurling grains of sand that would be pulled out to sea. The tides would retreat further, leaving the warmer waters of the Mediterranean for the Atlantic. Beyond were the Americas and the life Sebastian recently left.

They sat at a table and ordered espresso. He spoke, not knowing what else to say. He fingered the white porcelain of the cup uncertainly.

"You were never any good at this, being direct. There were always other things on your mind, too important to notice what mattered to anyone else. Old man Veillard. That's what they used to call you. Just like your father."

The masts of sailboats jutted toward the sky from moorings along the port. The collection looked a solitary forest, the sails furled tightly against the wind beating the lines before blue waves that rushed ashore.

"I went to South America. I needed to forget this place. There was too much confining me here. Everywhere I went, people had plans for me."

"I don't think you'll have that problem now."

"It's one of those things you don't appreciate until you've experienced it, going someplace where no one knows you. You have no past, no history. You can be anyone you want. It's liberating losing oneself."

"You shouldn't have come back. There's no one left who would want to see you."

The churn of hoary waves filled his ears as she spoke. "Everything has changed."

Light reflected off the metal chairs. Sebastian squinted at the glare and shifted his eyes toward the table. He saw a torn sugar packet, a white saucer, a stirrer with beads of coffee collecting in pools on the table, and Julía's hands folded one over the other. He studied the folds where her fingers bent, remembered their insistent touch, and wondered at how she applied polish to her nails. A banded sliver of pale skin encircled one of her fingers.

"You were married?"

"Married. Divorced. I don't know anyone who has lasting relationships."

"It makes you wish for better days, doesn't it?"

She inhaled deeply, tasting the air before she responded. "I don't know if there ever were better days, Sebastian. There were just days when we didn't know as much."

The two sat listening for the sounds of the sea they had heard in their youth.

Sebastian looked out over the dark liquid in his cup toward the sea, avoiding her eyes. "I don't know if I can face what happened here."

"Of course you can. You don't have any choice." The two stared in silence for a while longer as the inevitability of their situations set in. She broke their reveries with a few words. "People are going missing. They just disappear."

"More people than my father?"

"It's like an epidemic. Everyone has a story about someone close to them who just up and disappeared one day. Your father knew something about it though. He learned something about the disappearances. That's when he became erratic."

"Erratic?"

"No one had seen him in months. It wouldn't be the first time he became eccentric over the last year. I wasn't close to him anymore but someone has to look after him. He'd disappear for weeks. We found him sleeping at the site he was working on. The police laughed at me the first time I reported it. They keep pawning it off on each other. The city police say it's the regional police's jurisdiction. The regional police say they don't deal with missing persons. It's a labyrinth of excuses and negligence, a borgesian nightmare of bureaucratic red tape. Someone needs to pull it out of the stack of cases they already have. But I figure it's convenient for him to remain missing. I filed a report with the city police for what it's worth. They'll file it away until it's obsolete, but something needed to go on record."

Sebastian thought it odd for the two of them to remain close after he left. The man never approved of them. He could not imagine their relationship growing more intimate while he was away. "I thought you two stopped talking to each other."

"That was years ago, Sebastian. He was onto something. He knew things, things no one wanted to get out."

"Things like what? No one mentioned this to me."

"If you want to know about your father, come with me to the central police station tomorrow. I'll show you just what a mess things are."

She picked up her shoes by the straps and wandered down toward the beach. The sun's rays fell over her shoulders as she walked through the surf. Her body created a dark silhouette that was all he would ever see of her.

6

Waiting. The sounds of a dog barking echoed off stone walls. Iron latticed fixtures were attached to the walls of buildings along the crooked street. He stood in the soft light of afternoon near the address she had given. On one side 44 Calle de Duchamp, on the other 42. There was no 43. Even on the opposite side of the street the numbers read 60, 62, 66 and further on until Sebastian couldn't make out the digits. No odd numbers labeled the street. So Sebastian leaned on a black metal post designed to fend cars from the street and watched a dog that panted in the heat.

A tiled ceramic sign hung at the top of the entrance. It read 'birreria.'

Artists and knockoff dealers laid their wares on the flat stones of the square before the dry fountain. Handbags, sunglasses, shoes lined the top of display blankets. They looked more like bar graphs in neat stacks than products. Paintings stood at angles facing young girls and tourists who passed. Necklaces and bracelets glinted in the afternoon light. A lone guitar player strummed out songs while belting lyrics and smiling at any who would listen.

Sebastian counted time by watching the shadows from the posts creep along the sidewalk over the gutter. He counted tiles of the street until they stretched into a uniform blackness that blanketed the entire alley. It must be a strange thing, to be a shadow. One's life begins only when something comes between you and a source of light. You ply and bend as the other moves but ultimately you disappear without anyone noticing. He wondered how missing people felt, if they experienced the same notion, or if his father just vanished without realizing how strange it is to disappear from the world without any trace.

The city's central police building stood white and squat on an otherwise unremarkable street. On either side, apartments seven stories high rounded out the block. Lines of tall windows could be connected from the street in a crooked streak of glass running from building to building that reflected the opposite side of the street.

The regional police offices had been installed at the corner on the opposite side. Sebastian noted this as a new development. There must be some power sharing deal under way amongst the city and regional police forces. The regional police were an intermediary force designed to help the state achieve a more independent solution to policing the city. In addition to the city police, there were now state, regional, national, and park — all operating in the city.

Sebastian first went to the regional police building hoping to follow up on Julía's report. After an hour's wait they claimed to have no knowledge of the matter. They did, however, maintain that the city police offices across the street often held cases they did not cover.

Sebastian collected himself from the general inquiries window and the uniformed office there to thread his way across the street, dodging traffic as he went. A line of Nacionales were parked out front of the stations. Government subsidies gave the contract for police vehicles to a substandard domestic producer. They dubbed the line Nacionales. The cars were renowned for breaking down. They could not maintain their velocity in car chases. A joke among residents of the city was to race Nacionales on highways. The locals often won.

He mounted the stairs to the lobby. These places always needed some kind of structure to mark the entrance into some place more official than the street. Sebastian wondered at how he could design a government building if he was commissioned.

At the city police station, the attending officer claimed they had no knowledge of the report either.

"I'm following up on a report of a missing person."

"What's the name?"

"Hector Veillard."

The policeman typed on the keys of his computer. "No match. Is there another name?"

"Julía Reis filed a report here. There has to be a record."

"Look, our files go to the Central Archive to be stored. Maybe they got shipped there. You should check with them. They have centralized drives that back each other up. Ten or twelve of them. I hear they spend all day copying one drive to another. It's like a chain. If one link gets broken, there's another to back it up.

"Our system is being integrated with the Regional Police's database. We don't have access to a lot of data in the meantime. Some data has even been lost in the process."

"You'd think information would be more accessible with the new technology."

"Yeah, you'd think that wouldn't you? No one knows how to use the new system yet. We just integrated our database with the region's. We can't access any records. There's the hard copies in the vault at the Central Archive, but you need an Inspector's permission to go there."

"Can I see one?"

"Let me see." The uniformed man picked up the phone and asked for Inspector Torres to come out.

After a few minutes a tall man with a buzzed head, white shirt, and black necktie came out. He had a swagger about him that commanded respect from his fellow officers. Sebastian thought he was a man who was used to having people listen to him.

"I'm Inspector Torres. You wanted to see me?"

"I'm following up on a report that was made. There's no record of it here. I'd like to see the Central Archive."

"Come to my office."

His office was on the second floor with a view of the street in front of the station. Sebastian looked at the cars lined up in diagonal slants before the station. A desk stood in the center of the room. Stacks of folders and a desk lamp gave it a busy yet organized look. More files piled up in manila folders on the shelves behind and to the side of the inspector. Sebastian wondered if his father's report was in any of those stacks.

"No one knows their way around that place. Boxes were packed in with no order. You can have a look but I wouldn't bother."

A bottle broke through the inspector's window. Glass shattered and spread out onto his desk. The bottle knocked over an upright metal file rack and his desk lamp. The inspector jumped to his feet. "What the hell?" Inside the bottle an old rag had been stuffed down the neck and lit on fire. The files formerly arranged on his desk caught fire as the bottle rolled to a stop against them. The inspector hurried over to stamp out the mess. It took several angry stomps to put it out. The cuff of his pants caught fire too. He had to bat that out with his hands before he went to the window to see what was happening.

"Dogs!"

Sebastian approached the unbroken window next to where he sat. Outside he saw a few young men with bandanas or ski masks pulled over their faces. They ran away from the station, tipping over trash cans and hurling rocks as they retreated. A few beat cops beat the pavement after them, but they were slow and overweight.

"You better run!" the inspector screamed after them. "I'll kill you all when I find you!"

When the Inspector Torres barged out of the office, Sebastian realized his meeting was at an end. He hurried after the bellicose man throwing his weight around and pushing away anyone who got in his path on the way out. He barked orders to a few uniformed men on the way out. "I want squad cars circling a ten block radius. They won't get out of this net. All foot patrols are to commence down every street two at a time."

Outside the building, the inspector corralled his men into action.

The vandals had spray-painted a blue anarchy symbol on the roof and windows of a police car. The tires had been slashed so no one moved it. The other cars that were lined up in diagonal slots banged their bumpers against trashcans that had been hurled against their rear windows. The wire cans rattled backwards as the cars pulled out, distributing old newspapers and food wrappers into the street. The sirens lit up and howled.

Sebastian watched the blue lights disappear around the corner and reflect on the windows of an intersecting street as the cars pulled away. A hydrant had been knocked over in the chaos. Water spewed up into the air and splashed onto the street. The refuse from the trash cans floated along the current of water filling the curbside.

"Will somebody turn off the damn water main?" the inspector growled at the crowd of people milling before the station. Two uniformed officers hauled a man doubled over up the stairs. He wore bracelets on his arms behind his back. His eyes were red and tears fled down his face. They must have pepper sprayed him. "You're going to feel a lot worse than that before we're done with you," the inspector called to the man before they carted him inside. The prisoner's clothes were dirt-smeared and ragged. His hair was gnarled and dreaded. His bandana hung loosely about his neck. Who were these people, Sebastian wondered. He turned to survey the station as they hauled the captive in.

Several windows had been shattered. Flames spread up in a few of them, mostly on the first and second floors. He saw people hurrying to put out the fires inside the station. On the wall next to the staircase, *West* had been spray-painted in large letters. This word again appeared to Sebastian, first in his father's journal, now in the defiance of a group of anarchists attacking a police station. He tried to imagine how his father could be involved with a group of criminals. It was impossible to believe. Even with the ramblings in the journal, Sebastian could not see his father collaborating with a counter culture. The man had too much invested in the city to try and take it down. But the word *West* was the only tangible evidence he had between the disappearance of his father and the physical presence of the city. He had to follow it. He had to know more.

If the police caught some of the attackers, Sebastian wanted to know. He wanted to find out just who these dissenters were. Maybe then he would have a better idea of what happened to his father.

He tried to get the inspector's attention. "Inspector Torres, who are these people?"

He climbed into a squad car as he spoke. "They're dead men, that's who they are. No one vandalizes my station like that. No one."

The chaos spread further into the streets now. Sebastian imagined the net spreading wider out from the station.

*

The onset of evening cooled the air and Sebastian inhaled the breeze as it rushed in through the street.

Shutters pulled down in front of shops on the street. Graffiti artists' initials covered the ringed metal barrier. The names only appeared at night while everyone else slept during the day.

With reluctance, he admitted that Julía had stood him up, perhaps in some childish gesture of revenge. He wished he had never hurt her. She didn't deserve the suffering he saw in her eyes the day before. If a few hours of solitude meant she found some peace in her life, he was happy to give it. Sebastian resolved himself to leave, brushed his pant legs as he rose and ambled back toward the promenade. Maybe one day he would see her under more positive circumstances. Now everything seemed shit.

He wanted to search not just for Julía, but for that life Julía had always found for him. It must still be there, beneath the cracks of the city somewhere.

Sebastian felt more at ease as he ambled along the Promenade. While so much of the city had changed, it was impossible to affect a place that was so central to the life of the city.

The Promenade was the boundary between old and new cities. It was a part of all life here. True residents of the city were said to walk it once a day, balancing the space between old and new before finally seeing the sea at its mouth. The city spilled out from all sides into this human stream. The tributaries ran in from all sides, emptying their contents into the teeming mass. On one side, Gothic buildings stood bronze under the sun's light. Rambling alleys could be seen from glimpses to this side, providing an idea of the warren further within. On the other, large orderly blocks could be seen down the broad avenues which led to the promenade. These avenues were spaced at regular intervals, and were populated by rectangular buildings. They seemed cold and unrelenting to Sebastian because of their flat fronts and sides. He did not remember there being so many, but it had been a long time since he had been home.

The Promenade was a dried up riverbed that had been converted to a broad pedestrian avenue. It ran from one of the central plazas of the city to the sea. At one time, there had been a direct route from trade ships to the markets lining the Promenade. Now it was lined with shops of all kinds — restaurants, trinket shops, cafes, bakeries, jewelry stores, watch shops. There were three metro stops along its length. On one side was the Old Quarter, the other the Expansion. Nestled between the sea and the city center, it was an essential route in the city. Anyone going from one part of the city to another traversed it. It was said you were not truly from the city if you did not walk along the Promenade every day.

Ambling in every direction, as one had to among the crowd, he headed for the market. The market: its high roofed ceiling allowing light to pass through the corrugated plastic; its stacks of fruit colored red, green, yellow, orange; its fish and squid bedded in ice that melted with the day, down drains at the bottom of stalls; its corner cafes with round metallic bars and fixed padded stools upon which customers would slowly sip beer with their bocadillos.

Gossip from women with hair bleached from their love of the sun still chattered in his mind. The structures of his youth seemed all at once changed. Sebastian did not know what to make of them now. He navigated the narrow, illogical tributaries emptying into the Promenade. Its appearance seemed ever changing as the people passed along it. The old shops he remembered had faded into obscurity. Shiny, glittering, mammoth buildings replaced them with the newest wares from some other land. The visual cacophony was jarring, but his mind would be eased when he frequented the foundations of his youth. He set about reacquainting himself with the city from which he had long been absent.

He breathed in the fragrance of the sea's bounty, chilled in the afternoon air. It was not as fresh as he had remembered. There was a grid of stalls housed under a tall iron-wrought canopy.

Sebastian walked from the market, satisfied with himself, into the glaring light of the midday sun. It beat fiercely in the air. He noted shopkeepers were beginning to close their shops to avoid the brunt of the sun's fury. They would rest indoors for hours, safe from its fury. Sometimes these shops would not open again that day, leaving the unaware in need.

But now he wondered if life were different then. He had aged, and perhaps with age, changed his perspective through time. There was something more than age though. He noticed that for every shop that was closing, others were remaining open. They welcomed business, not caring about the heat. Sebastian wondered if they would remain open long into the night to cater to what weary souls who wandered under the midnight skies. Sebastian remarked that there were more of these shops as he came closer to the Promenade.

He left the market not disappointed because the sights and smells of the place reminded him of a life he had forgotten. He needed to find some purchase in this strange world.

He set out for home but as he wandered through the narrow streets, he became less sure of where he was heading. Sebastian had traveled these streets numerous times, but he could not recognize where he was. He wandered down one street after another, meeting intermittent squares and the occasional fountain — none of which looked familiar to him. This seemed to go on for hours into the night. He noticed couples hugging each other as they walked home at the end of the night. Cats rummaged through trash bins. Some stared at Sebastian eerily, their eyes catching the moon's light. Others hissed and scratched at each other as they fought for scraps. There was an odd couple embraced on the side of a street. A clatter of cans could be heard down one of the streets, but he could not tell which. The sound reverberated among the narrow paths.

He turned east and wandered along the fringe of the Old Quarter. His path led him through it, lazily recounting his youth running through the convoluted wandering streets. He had become lost many times as he first set out into them on his own. He remembered the fear he had first felt at losing his way, but as he wandered, he always inevitably wandered back to someone, or someplace he knew. It was not such an intimidating place then. The narrow corridors were full with familiar faces. They brimmed with an older way of life. He was disconcerted by his current surroundings, now populated more by refuse than rejoice.

It was odd that he could not find Julía. The address was the same yet there was no sign of her. The very structure of the building had changed. His father was missing, his friends disappearing, and buildings were changing over the course of a night. He wished the world were not so foreign to him. It was all he had left and it was vanishing before his very eyes.

He walked down the same streets he had walked the day before, but today everything was different. The old men on benches were gone. The stalls full of fruit and seafood had disappeared. In their place a mammoth building stood. It rose over a dozen stories in the air. Sebastian entered through glass sliding doors that opened as someone approached them.

Inside, the map of a department store greeted him. He smelled too many perfumes to differentiate between scents. Men's clothes, women's dresses, housewares, bedding, electronics, and even groceries moved past him in neat little shopping bags held by customers. The address was the same as yesterday, yet the place had changed.

Sebastian walked out to verify the numbers. They were the same. How could a place vanish overnight? Sebastian wondered. He walked up and down the promenade checking and rechecking the addresses of the surrounding buildings. 41, 43, 46, 49. They were all where they should be, yet the market he had seen yesterday was no more. He backed away from the gargantuan store, afraid its presence clouded his thought. He paused next to a crowd watching a street performer and eyed the faces of the spectators.

The hub of life was slowly eroding as the Expansion reached its even blocks and shiny shops within the Old Quarter's breast. There the establishments waited until their line could be advanced to replace the old, that without worth. Even on the sides met by the sea, where that credulous wash foamed upon the beaches, where worn stone steps climbed down to meet the tides carrying merchant ships, floating markets had encroached. Large freighters clouded the waters with oils. The murky depths were hardly livable. Not many bathed their spirits in the waters, much less ate what creatures survived within them.

Peals of laughter from the nearby table reached over Sebastian's ears. The woman made a show of appreciating something said by her companion. The sound rang false to Sebastian in its forcefulness. She expanded the show. "You can't really mean that. I can't imagine how you could ever come up with such an idea." The man with her stubbed out his cigarette as he leaned in to speak. "It's easy, once you have the right frame of mind." He eyed her wolfishly. Her laughter faded in the distance of the port. Waiters attended their tables. Children smoked from the boardwalk overlooking the beach. A few old men played dominoes in the space beneath. She put her hand on his and the two left.

The noise of traffic faded as he traversed the street too small for cars. The string of fabricated buildings ran along the curving street. As he walked, he noticed only the occasional stray. All else was silent. The buildings slowly lost color. They all ran one into another in a colorless white. Sebastian thought he could brush off the surface with his hand. He dragged it as he stepped, and wiped a chalk white mortar from his hands.

A few steps in front of him, something scurried in one of the side streets. A rat, no doubt, he thought as he passed by its opening. It was with great surprise that he noticed two small boys hiding against the wall. They were dirty and cringing, with rags for clothes and dirt smeared across their faces. Dark, intent, and filthy, they searched, stalking an intruder in their nest. He wondered what they were when the only other inhabitants of the day sprung from the darkness for his wallet. One launched himself onto Sebastian's chest and grabbed hold of his body, smiling all the while like a demon born of greed. The other darted around his legs and reached for the purse. Sebastian was in no mood to be preyed upon by these rats and tossed the first into a wall. The second was just extracting his wallet when Sebastian kicked him across the street. The two lay piled like beaten rugs still in need of cleaning. He retrieved his wallet from the cobbled street and wiped debris from his hands that flecked the streets.

So this was the depth to which his home had fallen. He clenched his fist and pounded the wall. Wasting mortar fell to the street and Sebastian walked home to what was left of his house.

He was more confused than ever after the night's events. Sebastian walked through the square to his house, reeling from the hour. The sun was beginning to peek over the roofs of the adjoining buildings. He squinted under it's light. All of his expectations were being turned on their sides and kicked through the streets. He didn't know what to make of any of it.

At the heart of the problems he had seen since his return, was absence. In the distance between individuals, he saw an absence of the familiar. There were no connections among those he saw. Relationships, whether trivial or deep-seated, missed an essential understanding between parties. People spoke but no one understood. Each person remained in solitude, not fully understanding the isolation of the other.

In this way no true communication was taking place in the city. It's true that people went about their everyday business, conducting affairs, commuting on trains, and visiting bakeries, but not one of the inhabitants of the city bridged the abyss between their isolated existences. It was a hole that was growing. With the absence of understanding, more were becoming isolated. Every day saw the withdrawal and eventual disappearance of another member of the city. As the abyss grew, individuals became enveloped by their isolation. Lives became menial affairs until they dwindled into the dull and vapid existence of the routine.

In a world like this, he had little chance of finding anything, much less so for exactly whom he was searching.

He stared at the numbers on Grey's card. They were little and meaningless. How could something so small change anything, he thought. Out of everything he had seen, these few digits allowed the only avenue for the secret to his lost past. He lifted his phone and dialed.

II

The small hours of night receded into morning as dark blue hues bled into a weak orange that brimmed on the horizon. The sea looked a welcome sight to Sebastian from the truck in which he rode. His guide had driven out of the small confines of the Old Quarter toward the open expanse of the sea. The truck stopped facing a floating pavilion before turning to follow the water. Sebastian breathed the salt air in, deeply. Images of the night ran through his head as they drove along a highway that ran parallel to the shore. Sebastian turned his head to follow the line where earth and water met as they drove. Tall palms passed as he stared off at the sleepy shore, where the elderly strolled and delivery men dropped off food for markets. The orange morning light drove most of the nightlife from the street though a few stragglers could be seen. They walked wearily with uncertain steps and loud voices that interrupted the morning calm. Scintillating colors dappled on the water. Forms on the boardwalk and beach had a hazy quality to them in such a bright display. Sebastian felt uncertain they existed. He imagined being one of those old men, wandering the shore in the morning, with nothing to do but amble along with the day. He preferred their life to his own that day.

He leaned back into the seat, which creaked as he did so. He peered out at the cranes and their arms reaching over the cityscape, a mix of bronze, faded red, and ecru hues. Along the beach during the summer, large umbrellas stood in the sand shielding men in short bathing suits; women, some topless, some in bikinis, laid out on towels from end to end in a myriad of bright blues, pinks, yellows, and reds that ran as far as he could see until the beach disappeared and larger cargo freights obscured the shore. Only the freights could be seen now.

Overhead balcony after balcony towered, some with linens draped over the edge dappling with the short breezes that pushed in from the avenue at the end of the street. The white lines swayed lazily as if even the clothes were in no hurry to dry despite the heat.

The highway emptied Sebastian and the driver into an industrial district separated from the Old Quarter. Large cranes and squat warehouses filled the skyline. Everything was built to house and transport cargo delivered by ships that docked nearby. The sea disappeared. The wired arms of cranes and cargo containers stacked one on top of another formed an impressive wall, beyond which, water still pulsed ashore apart from Sebastian's view. The industrial district had grown since Sebastian returned. He did not remember it being so possessive of the landscape it occupied. Even stranger was that Sebastian did not see anyone as they drove. The industrial town was devoid of life. Even rats were scarce as they drove between warehouses that could house numerous trailers. The driver turned in between two stacks of cargo containers. The containers rose up as far as Sebastian could see above him in muted reds, blues, and whites. They met intersections among the containers and the driver took Sebastian deeper into the district. It seemed a maze of cargo. Sebastian thought he would be at a loss to escape from this place if he had to. He adjusted his position in the passenger seat as the shade from the cargo freights overtook the truck. The leather creaked as he fell deeper into the seat. The driver paid no attention to Sebastian. He turned the truck in between two stacks of cargo containers. His hands gripped the black ridges of the wheel and he bounced with the vibrations of the truck as if he were part of the vehicle.

"We're going to meet a ship?"

"We're going where we're told to go." The driver resumed his silence. He kept his eyes on the lane before him, never veering toward Sebastian.

59

A feeling of being cloistered crept over Sebastian as they turned from one lane between containers into another. They met intersections among the containers and the driver took Sebastian deeper into the industrial district. A vast network of lanes unfurled before Sebastian. He tried to make a mental map but the lanes were too identical. The patchwork of muted reds, blues and whites seemed endless. The numbers and letters on each container held no meaning for him. He looked out the window to the sky above. A rectangle of blue mirrored the cement on which they drove. It seemed a soft canopy too far for him to reach. Gulls floated in the sea breeze above, held aloft by currents that never reached the maze of cargo freights. Sebastian felt only the rush of displaced air as the truck zipped past warehouses large enough to house several dozen containers. Not a soul walked in the empty maze of containers. Not even rats moved as they drove between warehouses with heavy metal doors bolted shut.

"You ever get lost in here?"

The driver grimaced. "The containers move. Every few days you have to find a new way in."

"You don't know where we're going?"

"There's too much freight traffic. They're constantly rearranging things." The truck rounded another corner of four containers stacked high. "Here we are."

The maze of containers diminished behind them as the wheels of the truck propelled them along the cement expanse. The arm of a crane dangled a container taken from a ship docked at the edge of the quay. It swung slowly. The weight of the box dragged in the air as the arm rotated. When the arm stopped, all the men milling about the scene watched as the weight of the container slowly swung forward with the momentum of the crane. They waved to the operator for him to lower the freight onto a truck waiting in a line that led up to the ship. Once secure, these trucks sped off into the maze of containers. To where, Sebastian had no idea. He saw none of them on the way in.

They parked to the side of the commotion and walked toward a group of men discussing something fervently. Seagulls floated on the currents of wind above. Sebastian shielded his eyes. The gulls' wings formed into a W as they coasted lazily back and forth in the air above. The men stared and pointed at a blueprint unfurled in their midst. Sebastian could see fingers depress points in the paper as he approached.

"This is him," the driver said.

The one holding the blueprint looked up. He wore glasses, a shirt tucked tightly into his jeans with a belt, and a neon yellow hardhat. "You? Who is this?"

The smell of industrial dust was stirred into the air, either by the sea of some lorry passing by. Redolent with iron filaments, the odor made Sebastian's nose twitch. He averted his head to avoid choking in more debris. The foreman broadened his nostrils to take it in, as if the iron gratings from the crane invigorated him.

"What do you want with me?" Sebastian said.

"We don't want you. Why did you bring him here?"

"I was told," the driver said.

"Who told you? This is a problem."

The man holding the blueprints stepped in. "Listen, we need him." The foreman and the man with glasses walked off to discuss the issue. A few bulldozers and a crane were positioned along the block. The crane swung and its ball clumsily laid bare the insides of one of the houses in line. The others were in either more or less advanced states of disrepair. In the more advanced cases, bulldozers had picked clean the insides of the house, leaving only a hollow shell of walls without a roof or floors. Even further along, Sebastian saw machines excavating the foundation of former houses. These machines dug deeper into the earth than the previous builders had. Whoever was coordinating the work of the machines had decided to join the lots together. Where one house had stood, an earthen ramp had been built so that other machines could descend into the adjoining lots and dig the block even deeper.

They returned.

"I don't care what he said."

Sebastian looked from the excavation site to the few remaining houses at the other end of the block. Sebastian knew that these, too, would be engulfed by the gaping chasm that dug deeper into the ground. These, too, would be engulfed by absence.

The workers began shouting. A freight dropped on the side of the lorry. The truck fell to its side. The windows smashed against the concrete. The metal handle securing the cargo door broke, and the door swung open with a loud creak. People began to crowd around the accident. Sebastian thought he saw a gaunt arm and set of legs emerge from the container before feeling a dull impact at the back of his skull and everything went dark.

2

Voices whispered somewhere close by. They spoke in rushed tones assaulting and parrying one another while Sebastian lay down. He wondered if it were him they discussed.

Sunlight drenched his body. His hand twitched and brushed against some kind of fabric. Warmth called to him through closed eyelids. He saw specks of light darting about as his consciousness returned. His cheek pressed against something firm and cool on one side. The contours of his face became warm and malleable on the other. He ran his hand along his cheek and rubbed under his eye. His bones ached. He pushed himself up into a world of blinding light. He shielded his face with one arm. He hadn't fallen asleep here.

He lay in a bed, whose he did not know. He stepped falteringly from it. Everything was too bright. He could make out nothing. He thought he was in a room. Light came in through a set of glass doors. He could make out forms a shade lighter than the bright expanse he found himself in. His limbs jerked when he thought to move. Tears fled his eyes as his irises dilated to become accustomed to the light. He inhaled sharply. As he moved, trying to take in the room, he stubbed his toe against a nearby chair. He fell. Cold tile met his face. His vision began to focus and made out a blue floral pattern lining the piece next to his cheek. A door opened at the edge of his vision. He saw only the laces on a pair of shoes and the hazy pants legs leading up from them.

"We were wondering when you were going to wake up."

"How did I get here?"

"Be calm. You fell hard."

"There were people."

"You may have an injury. You may not be recalling things correctly. We'll have someone take a look at that. What else did you imagine while you were out?"

Sebastian pushed himself up back to the couch. The person pulled metal shutters down to block out the afternoon light. The sound of metal running through its track echoed off the walls of the room. Small bolts of light streamed in through small slats in the metal shutters. The scant beams warmed Sebastian's cheek as they moved across the room. He thought he heard voices in the adjoining room. His vision became clearer. He sat up slowly. His head felt afloat, his neck stiff, but everything else seemed fine. To the outside observer, the pallor of his skin had whitened.

Before him stood a woman who wore a neat blazer and skirt, and freshly ironed blouse open at the neck. Her glasses fit snugly around her eyes. Her hair fell just past her chin in a neatly cut fashion.

"Who are you?"

"Please, Mr. Veillard, be calm. I sent the letter requesting you return. Xavi couldn't send it himself, for obvious reasons."

"He doesn't know anything about a letter. I asked him days ago. Said it must be some fabrication."

"As someone who looks after the details of his life, I found it was in his best interests. He's miserable, you see. He can't even admit it to himself. I have to take care of so many things for him. This is just one more."

Sebastian searched around the room. "Who are you? How did you bring me here?"

"He hasn't been able to look after himself for some time now. Xavi attracts a specific element that never seems to leave, even when they're unwanted. I look after him. More importantly, he wants your help, so I'm here to look after you."

Sebastian rubbed the back of his head. He touched the swelling base of his skull gingerly. He looked about the room for the door. The metal shutters closed him in on one side. The wall behind him and to his right held no doors. The only exit stood behind the woman who had brought him to this room so far removed from anything recognizable.

"You're not listening to me. I've had enough of this. I'm leaving." Sebastian rose to walk past her. Blood rose to his head quickly and he faltered.

The woman reached out to brace him. "You had quite a fall. Be careful. If you leave now you'll never find out what happens to people in this city. Your father is included in that."

"You want me to help you when everything I ever cared about is dissipating into the air like smoke? I don't even know who you are. No one can be found now. It's like they never existed."

"People disappear because they want to, Mr. Veillard. Let me explain."

She drew him to a desk situated near the entryway. On it porcelain cups on small saucers lay atop the wooden grain of the desktop. She poured coffee for the two of them as he collected his thoughts. The events of the morning unfolded in his head. He tried to understand how it all came together, but realized he could do nothing but wait for her to continue.

She hesitated. Sebastian noticed because every fiber of her body looked as if it had purpose. She tucked her hair neatly to her head. Her glasses fit snugly around her eyes, nose and ears. Even her jacket seemed as if it were placed in the exact location to emphasize her shoulders. When she opened her mouth and nothing came out, she averted her eyes as if the words disappeared before she could utter them. "Xavi didn't used to be like this. There was a time when he functioned very well in his position. He never went to excess, not then. It was only after that, that, well…"

"I've seen him."

She grabbed a cup of coffee by the handle and turned it on the plate, hesitating a few seconds before drinking. "Yes, we all have. Xavi came to me at a point in my life when I needed help. He was kind to me and gave me the opportunity to work with him. He looked out for me. He didn't have to. He's been very kind when no one else was. You have to help him leave. He'll die if you don't."

"Die? I thought he's doing well."

"There's no one else he trusts. You see, he would leave if he could, but he's accumulated so much debt that it's impossible for him. They own him. Nothing he does is of his own accord. He just does what he's told."

"You think he'll come with you?"

"He'll come. He'll come because he won't survive otherwise. He knows this."

"You don't need me for that."

"With you around, no one will notice that Xavi is gone. The people at his apartment hardly know he is there anyway. I've often suggested he find another, one that no one knows about. Keep asking questions."

"No one tells me anything. You won't even tell me why you sent the letter."

"I've already told you."

"You told me what you wanted me to hear."

"You changed things. Just by being here. No one expected you back. How could you not notice? Doors opened for you in the past few days that it takes others years to find. You live a charmed life, Mr. Veillard."

"I haven't done anything. Why couldn't he ask me?"

"His pride. He still resents you. Please, for his sake. I can't make you do this. In fact, Xavi can't even ask you himself. You have to trust me. He wants you to help him. He wants to leave badly, but he can't ask you. You will have to do this out of respect for the man he once was. Please consider this. After all, he did bring you here from the industrial district."

"I saw people in the containers at the dock."

66

She paused. Her eyes looked to the ground. Her lips became tight. "We all see things these days. Your father's not dead. He disappeared, like the rest. I can't tell you much more, but he's not the only one. It's become a sensation in the city."

"How do you know he's alive?"

She paused. "There have been sightings. The dead come back, but no one sees them for long. I'm worried about Xavi. He might be next. He's been erratic, like the others."

Sebastian remembered the gaunt limbs from the cargo freights. They were emaciated, not like those of Xavi's companion. Skin hung loosely from the bones. Xavi's assistant had no intention of revealing to him anything about the strange happenings at the port, the labyrinth of freight containers, the people inside, but she could be able to gain him entrance to the world in which his father was involved. He needed to follow her deeper along the line of her reasoning. "What do you want me to do?"

"I want you to pick something up for Xavi. It's for him, not me. It will help him leave the city. Otherwise, something will happen to him. I'm sure of it." She handed him a note folded in half. "I can't be seen going there. People will know. Once you get it, come directly to me."

"What is it?"

"You're better off not knowing."

*

On the way out, he passed through a living room decorated neatly with a few couches and tables. Light filtered past the city skyline through broad windows lining the wall to his left. Sebastian counted a few of the spires on gothic cathedrals near the Old Quarter. Buildings erected in his absence obstructed many of the spires he knew. The obstructions were large, rectangular boxes. A cold glow reflected on the windows hiding any hint of the insides.

The cathedral spire no longer rose from the depths of the Old Quarter. The day before he had walked past it. Now it was gone. He had seen it the day before. The arms of cranes reached into the old quarter from the expansion. He counted off the department stores near the Parc Ciudad, the open space of the Promenade between the old quarter and El Raval, the old roman fort, and Xavi's office in the Expansion in the distance, but he saw no cathedral. It had disappeared. The crane's arm stood too far away to have demolished it. The building had just vanished, as if part of a movie set that could be switched in an afternoon for the next scene.

*

He stopped by a convenience store lighting up the night with its open glass windows and fluorescent lights on the way home. A few groceries were all he needed. It had been days since he had bought anything. He walked out with a bag crinkling in his arms. Outside it almost felt like day in the convenience store's light. A rectangle of light emanated from the shop into the street. Beyond, streetlights did a spotty job of marking the way home for him.

He mounted the stairs to his building and fumbled with his keys. Before he could find the right one, he looked up. A woman sat on the steps to his house. She was tall with dark wavy hair and wore a cotton skirt and a white camisole with spaghetti straps. "I waited all afternoon." He climbed the stoop with the paper bag of groceries cradled in one arm. At the top he stopped.

Julía said nothing, just walked up, pulled him close and kissed him fully on the lips. She stepped back and looked into him, weighing what she found. He pulled keys out of his pocket and inserted them into the lock. The door swung open. She entered, pulling her white camisole shirt off over her shoulders, and tossed it to the floor. She looked back at Sebastian still standing in the doorway and tugged her skirt down. She stepped up the staircase wearing only her panties, her fingers lightly touching the banister as it curled up into the floor above. He watched her white tipped nails glide along and followed her arm up to her face that watched him expectantly. Her head disappeared upstairs and he watched her bare feet picking their way gingerly. He unbuttoned his shirt and closed the door, tossing it aside as he entered. The bag of groceries fell to the floor and an orange rolled out onto the floorboards.

3

Notions of the life ahead filled his mind during the night. He looked past the shutters to the sky hoping to find some stars. It was empty, a sheet of blue, hazy with light polluted from the city. A sliver of moon hid behind the haze peeking out as wind blew the cloudy sky in from the sea.

He held her, nestling his face in the side of her neck where he inhaled deeply. Her scent invigorated him: a sweet smell with a touch of perspiration that clung to her dark hair. He rubbed his face in these strands and an absolution washed over him.

Their conversation was dwindling with their exhaustion. They sat in silence watching the dawn come into existence. She had watched from the rooftop as the lights from the night became obscured. In the tired breath of dawn, she marveled at this new world.

The sounds of people rising drifted over from somewhere in the background. The spent, grumbling of their voices trailed along the morning's line like notes played in the air. She listened to the maladroit stumbling. Doors opened, shutters were flung, and the hush of linens released their embrace of the day's occupants. She was almost lulled to sleep by the beauty of it all.

"There's nothing quite like it, is there?"

She was staring off, lost in this world.

They sat quietly as the sun rose full into the sky. He decided he should sleep before all this beauty overwhelmed him.

Together, they walked inside. He slowly watched her barefoot shadow, that had come into existence with the dawn, grow larger until it vanished inside the apartment. She fell into the first furniture they found and dreamt of all the sunrises yet to come.

In the morning, his notions of freedom seemed childish. Nothing would change. If anything, his attempt to reclaim parts of his life from the past represented how utterly futile it would be to recreate something lost, or rather forgotten. No part of him was the same as that of the boy who left the city years ago. He was a new man. His night carried a respite from the present, a brief jump to the past where he forgot how utterly lost he had become in the landscape of the city. He should have been happy. Most exalt when they attempt to make goals in life. Even more celebrate when those goals are actually achieved. Sebastian was one of the few who had set a purpose for his life and actually met it; he had created a new life for himself, one that had no vestige of the old in it. Yet now he found himself toying with the idea of a forlorn past, one that he could live again. Notions like these drew him toward a precipice upon which he found himself walking. He had to decide between leaving his life free of a history and rejoining one into which he fit as part of a jigsaw puzzle, his piece defined by context.

Still, he thought, I must play the part. He propped his head up on one elbow to look at Julía. She slept. Her eyes closed, her back straight, she seemed posed like a doll cast aside. Her arms stretched as she stirred. Sebastian had to dodge one blow shooting out toward his chin. Then all at once, both eyes opened. She reached for a cigarette and lit up in bed. Sebastian felt happy to see her living in the same space as him again. It brought fond memories to him.

"This is nice."

"Yes."

"Part of me has missed mornings like this."

"They happen."

"It's not the same though. There's something different about you."

"What do you mean?" She arched her head toward him after a long pull.

"You. You're just different. There's no one quite like you."

She pondered this for a moment. "Thank you."

Sebastian pulled her close by her waist. "Breakfast. You like eggs. I'll make some."

"No."

"No?"

"No. I don't like eggs."

"What do you mean?" He had risen. "Of course you do."

"No. No eggs."

"You used to love them."

"No, I didn't. They're kind of disgusting, undeveloped embyos? Besides, I'm vegan."

Strange how some people change over time — their tastes, their looks, even their postures can take on new forms.

"What did you want to tell me the other day?"

She looked at him nonplussed.

"You said people are going missing."

"I can't remember."

"Xavi wants my help. He wants to leave. Does that have anything to do with it?"

"Who's Xavi?"

"Julía, stop acting."

She drew another drag from the pillow. "Who's Julía?"

This confused Sebastian. The night before, he met Julía at the door to his house, took her inside, and had sex with her through the night. Now, this woman, the same he took into his home, claimed she was not the woman he knew.

"If you're not Julía, then who are you?

"I'm Opal."

This was obviously some game. She played the part of the inconnu in his bed and he the beneficiary of a woman liberated from traditional notions of sexuality. Did she have to know him? No. She could do as she liked. Sebastian played through the game in his head. But he still could not find out why she would play another role other than to make him endure the same suffering she had when he left. He played along, delaying his questions.

"Fine. You're not Julía. You're Opal. So tell me, Opal. Why are you here?"

"You looked nice. Do I need a reason to go after a man who looks nice?"

"No, but … you never did this in the past. Why now?"

"Until last night, I had never seen you before. It would be hard to have memories of someone if you've never met them before, wouldn't it?"

"But, you look exactly like her."

"I can't say whether I do or do not look like her. I have no frame of reference."

"Ok. Enough."

She pulled on her cigarette one last time and stubbed it out on the end table next to her. Smoke rose from the smoldering ember as she leaned back into the pillow. "Every seven years we have completely new bodies. They regenerate, you see? The cells become new again. The millions of tiny pieces of your pinky, the bone and tendon underneath, even the striations of color in your iris; all of them are duplicates of the original. As you get older, the cells make duplicates of duplicates. It's dna. Or rna. I forget which. You're literally a whole new person every seven years."

"That's insane. What are you telling me? I wouldn't remember anything if that were true. I don't care if you are Julía's double. You're lying. This is all a joke on me. You hate me that much."

"We're lucky. Memories are coded in the tissue of the brain. When everything starts anew, the cells just pull from the code and everything is reset. I'd like some mineral water. You?"

"Unbelievable. I didn't change. I can't. Everything that's happened won't leave me alone. No matter where I go or what I do. He's still with me, you see?"

"I'm hungry. Let's go out."

Sebastian stood up pulling the sheet with him. He stopped to consider the likelihood — in a city of a few million people scattered in the streets and housing leading from the sea up the hills — of encountering one who looked *exactly* like someone previously in his life, and not just at random, as if he caught a passing glimpse of her in the street, but encountering her in his home; a place the two of them had spent many nights furtively knowing the skin of their bodies while his parents chopped tomatoes for soup or filed books alphabetically; there were too many coincidences of this strange occurrence of doubling to be true for Sebastian's thinking. "If you're not her, why are you here?"

The double Opal put on her panties, stockings, then her skirt. She put on her camisole and gathered her things to leave. She tousled his hair as she was putting on her shirt.

She walked out the door. He followed this strange enigma, this doppleganger in his life. Maybe this was the phenomenon she told him about earlier. People going missing, just like this. Maybe they didn't go missing. They just forgot, he thought.

*

Julía climbed along a jetty, picking her way among the rocks, one foot claiming its hold after another. Her hair tousled in the wind blowing off the sea. Dark tresses crossed her forehead and she had to draw them back with a finger. The hoary rush of waves filled the seascape Sebastian took in as he filtered sand through his hands, grain by grain. He rolled a handful slowly in his palm, feeling the wet particles clump together and fall. A thin layer coated around the outside of his palm. The drier elements fell back to the shore, or blew away in the wind. Julía hopped to a rock further out and stared down into the water. She must be caught by her reflection, he thought. A modern day Narcissus. Or maybe a school of fish pecked at algae and other organisms living off the jetty. It must be like a natural reef where the smaller life of the sea could find harbor. Oysters and scallops could be buried between the rocks, piled to slow the erosion of the waves. Sebastian imagined tiny shrimp floating and fish that gulped them down whole with one swift intake of seawater.

She pulled her hair behind one ear as she looked. If she were captivated, she would never move, forever transfixed by the scene below. What she saw, Sebastian would never know. But the mysteries of her psyche remained locked to him behind distance and sea.

Beyond the rock jetty, extending out a hundred meters into the sea, the arm of a crane stood crooked in the horizon. The metal, painted red, stood on a plateau of the old port. It formed a right angle, first reaching up then out over the waves. The sun drew closer to the shore, and a hazy line of orange and purple began to blur the picture. The water looked still further out, beyond more jetties leading up to the crane. He saw a dappled version of the scene; the red crane reaching down, arm extended on the sea; except the arm was crooked, bending with the motion of the sea. The sun blushed the water with its orange light and a row of old warehouses resembling the staggered rooftops of houses completed the inversion of the scene above. Sebastian leaned, his hands digging into the sand as he placed the weight of his torso backward. Even here the city looked a mess, one contorted image after another of forgotten worlds and doubled images.

He could not shake the earlier revelation Julía really believed she was Opal. She was not the person he knew. Her absolute certainty on this point confounded all logic. If she were an exact double, how could he find her in his life, playing a similar role. And still, he had no idea why she came to him, found him among all the inhabitants of the city. He clung to her in the hope of finding some answer to this strange city that welcomed him into its contorted image of the place he once inhabited.

*

"Are you through with your little game yet?"

"What game?" She looked at him innocently, head tilted to one side as if he were the stranger in this situation.

"Why did you arrange to meet me, then not show up?"

"There's all kinds of reasons to lose yourself. You can imagine that, can't you?"

He thought about his father and how he had to release everything he accumulated in life and hope it all stood and did not fall, as so many things do once loosed in the world. For that man had failed, as Sebastian saw when he watched Julía standing still as water rushed upon the shore and splashed the backs of her calves. She bore no recognition of anything that he had done and she was one of his stalwart admirers, even when Sebastian and he argued. It was as if the man never existed and part of Sebastian enjoyed the little triumph he had been denied. He had left the country to avoid the overarching reach of the old man, and now that he had returned Sebastian could see the cracks in the foundation of what his father had constructed as his image. It all fell apart and was forgotten so quickly.

A small amount of guilt rose in him that he should not mourn the dead, but there were complications to their relationship. Julía ran toward and from the waves, laughing as she danced around the waves. How carefree she looked. The city Sebastian remembered was falling apart and she laughed. Maybe she was accustomed to it, having lived amid the changing landscape while he was away, but she truly seemed a different person than the one he met a few days ago. Her new name might be more appropriate for this strange person frolicking in the sea as if nothing had happened. Sebastian was uncertain if he should exalt or regret the change. So much baggage had been jettisoned, yet those same constraints were what made him. It was a growing freedom that made him feel a bit giddy watching the waves come ashore. He could do anything, be anyone. The sensation reminded him of his first days in South America, before the memory of his father crept upon him, making him realize it would not be so easy to escape. It took years to push the man from his thoughts, and now he was drawn into a world marked by his absence so strongly that none of it seemed right. He had to ask Julía. He had to know why the giddy feeling of being on the brink of something new was still moored to a memory, one that no one else seemed to remember.

The feeling had been liberating, leaving one's past behind. She said they should go to the train station to see what people looked like as they went from one place to another. He delayed his questions longer, seduced by the sensation he had all those years ago. He wanted to experience it again, to come closer to the impetus that drove him away to take hold of something that was still tangible in this city. So much had changed he had trouble reconciling the boy he once was — the one who had a history in the city — with the man who returned to a city in shambles, constantly changing, not a sleepy urban center by the shore.

He followed the urge to jump. The precipice upon which he stood invigorated him. Sebastian chose not to question her further and instead let her lead him through the city as she saw it. He wanted to forget. She seemed to know the city that was almost unrecognizable to Sebastian. In her lead, he could forget everything that was lost, both in his house and in the lives he had abandoned years earlier.

She caressed him as breezes do from time to time. In her lips, he tasted the sea. The purse of her lips pressed upon his evoked the rhythm of their bodies. They had watched waves wash upon the shore to deposit grains of sand from beds of far off places. Somewhere beyond, in the horizon, unknown, she had sensed that the blue mass existed. Beyond the smell of churros and coffee hanging in the air, mingling with the shuffling of newspapers, she heard the sea in the plodding steps of heels upon marble. It resonated, unrecognizable around her, except in the form before a scintillating slope of glass panes that provided her first view of the city beyond.

She stood motionless, staring up at the light with a transfixed look on her face. That face, the facile flash of ease, was a thing of dreams to him. She beguiled everyone surrounding her. The sun's rays washed over him. Even businessmen slowed their strides and reflected on the shimmer of light falling fantastically around their shadows. She had a presence all her own. Those passing close to her seemed drawn into orbit. Transfixed, as if shortsighted, they all were awakened to the minutia of a moment's passing. A million suns twinkled about his being but they all just hinted at something else, more elusive.

Her hair whisked lightly in his presence. He continued staring out through the sloping windows in disbelief. His vision arrested. Tiny beads caught in the glass of windows streaked aurous bars across his sight. Crimson began to fleck his cheeks as the world swung back into motion. The clop of suits' heels clattered. Coffee was poured into short white cups. Children waited and newspapers shuffled. She was enveloped by the crowd. The constant chatter of the train station slowly crept back into his senses, and as he looked around recognizing his surroundings, he found her gone.

The nettles in his spine tingled with a sensation he could not explain. There had been girls, and women, in his life. Some were intriguing, some forgotten, but none so memorable as this woman. She made him feel frightened and alive. Even the specks of dust, floating in the light, tinged with smoke, moved with a cosmic grace he never noticed.

She stirred. Her gaze fell from lofty contemplation to land directly on him. With lazy, dallying strides she approached. This woman, so at ease in the crowd, seemed more a gust of wind than someone causing his breath to become caught in his throat with each step. Thoughts of witticisms, smiles and laughs raced through him. He imagined how he would posture himself in order to keep her close.

"Tell me again how you're not Julía."

She kicked sand with her toes. "I'm a double. A doppelganger, see? I look just like the woman you know. Only I'm different."

"I still don't one hundred percent believe you. Doubles don't exist."

"Of course they do. It's all in your head. You see what you want to see. You miss her and you just met me so I become her in your mind."

"Whenever you want to stop playing this game, let me know. It would be nice to call you by your name again. We should go home."

"What is a home? No one knows anymore. Too many residents have sold what little they had to cash in. It's an unequal exchange. The wealth they are trading … it's material. There are finite things in this world. Material wealth is one of them. What did they get in exchange? An *idea* of wealth. There is little tangible about it. Currency only has value when people agree on its worth. In itself, it means nothing without that agreement. Currency does not create a home. The tangible things — property, oil, water, land —

these will always have value. It's what we make of them that matters, not what you get for them.

"I fear that people have forgotten how to make homes for themselves, not just buildings but homes in which we live. That's causing people to forget. They no longer have the idea of how to create a space that is *habitable*. It's something we've lost along the way."

"That's it. We need to take you to a doctor."

4

Sebastian saw people crowding into a medical clinic in the Old Quarter. As he got closer he noticed someone he knew.

"Inspector?"

"Veillard. I thought I should see you here."

"What are you doing?"

"It's my daughter. She needs help. She doesn't see anymore. I try reading to her. The pictures used to help. Now she just stares off at the wall. I don't think she even knows I'm the one who is reading."

Sebastian looked at the girl. The Inspector held her hand. His massive paw dwarfed her small fingers. Sebastian wondered that the man could be so delicate. His meaty hands could crush her. The girl's eyes were wide. They looked blankly at the wall. Sebastian leaned down to look into her face. The girl's irises didn't flicker. She stared, registering nothing.

"Some people at the station who work in missing persons have had some success with this doctor. No one talks about it. We can't even acknowledge it at the station." The inspector averted his gaze. "This doesn't exist, but people look for answers. They look for *ways*. A few of the missing people have been found, but the state, the state they're in. This doctor sounds like a hypnotist to me. You hear about him around corners. The conversation stops after you pour a coffee. A sort of ghost whisperer. Whispering is the only thing she hears these days. What else could I do?" He squeezed her hand gently and patted her hair. "It's an epidemic."

"An epidemic? What do you mean?"

"I couldn't tell you about it at work. My job, it prevents me from officially saying anything. But you see what I'm going through. People are losing their memories.

They wake up one day and forget who they are. Just like my little one."

Julía bent down folding her hands over her sundress. "That's a pretty doll."

"Thank you."

"What's your name?"

"Isidora."

Inspector Torres pulled his lips tight. "She's Mercedes. She made Isidora up. Insists on it now. That's one of the symptoms."

"That's a pretty name." Julía turned to Sebastian. "Let's go to the shore."

"We were just there, Julía."

"I'm Opal."

Sebastian was taken aback. "Stop it."

"She suffers from it too? Come inside with me. You'll see. This man knows about the epidemic."

*

They went to the doctor's office via the stairs. The elevator was out of service. The Inspector labored away, a sheen of sweat developing as he climbed. Julía and Sebastian followed behind the Inspector's daughter, who trailed and clutched a doll in one arm. Sebastian was not certain to trust the Inspector after the scene in the street. It was unclear exactly what was happening in the city and he had no idea why he followed the man other than mystery. Sebastian thought it was some kind of game. He thought Julía was playing with him after having left her for so long. Could this be real? His father seemed to suffer too. What if he underwent the same changes? No one seemed to know up from down in the city. The Inspector led him toward the unknown, but an unknown with a promise of an answer. Sebastian tightened his grip on the railing as he ascended.

They entered the doctor's office into a waiting room. Before them two rows of chairs lined the walls leading up to a reception desk and a door behind it off to the side. Twenty or so people sat in wooden chairs with padded seats. Warm lighting filled the room from strategically placed lamps. The place reminded Sebastian of Grey's save that it seemed a mirror image. Where Grey's felt sterile, this place had a warm air about it.

The Inspector led Sebastian between the two rows to check in with the receptionist. Curious, these rows, thought Sebastian. Why the parallels? His eyes examined both rows of patients as he traversed between them. Many read magazines. Others sat worriedly shifting in their seats. Inspector Torres' tone seemed meek compared to his shouts in the street earlier. Sebastian wondered at how the man could be so different. The Inspector cradled his daughter's head as she peeked up to the reception desk. An exchange between the Inspector and the receptionist led to both Sebastian and the Inspector being handed clipboards with paperwork to be completed.

They returned between the rows. One of two of the patients eyed the newcomers as they traversed the empty space in the middle of the waiting room. Sebastian sat with Julía next to a fern. The Inspector and his daughter found a place across the aisle separating the two rows. He touched the leaves of the fern between his fingers. Moisture collected under the leaves. Sebastian rubbed his fingers and looked down to a pile of old magazines. An aloof companion accompanied each of the anxious. These aloof individuals seemed less concerned about their stay in the waiting room of the doctor's office. The aisle between the rows did not bother them, as it was beginning to for Sebastian. He shifted and looked at Julía who was unconcerned. Despite the warm air, these rows pointed at something. They led to that inevitable door, through which Sebastian had no idea what to expect. If this doctor had solutions to Julía's recent amnesia, why were there so many? The legs of Mercedes dangled from the chair. An occasional twitch moved them off kilter from the pendulum swings. They began to sway slightly after the tremor.

"Ideas … bah." The Inspector waved his hand as if to brush the words out of the air. "What use are ideas? Do you hurt, little one?" He patted his daughter's leg. She looked up to his imploring face blankly. "Ideas are worthless. We toss them aside when something important comes along. Isn't that right, little one?" The girl nodded. He tightened his lips and grimaced. He pulled her cap on straight and continued with an exhalation. "No one has the luxury of having ideas any more. Whatever we believed in: the right, the left, wealth, justice — it's all crap in the pot. Toss it in without a care in the world and see what happens. Sebastian, it's just a game. People play with what you believe in. The only way to win is to give up. Throw your hands in the air." The Inspector patted both his knees and raised his palms. "I've shortened my sights on what matters." He looked to his side. "Family. Even this is fading."

Sebastian leafed through the pages of paperwork on the clipboard. He looked over the lines of black ink on the white paper. They appeared in different sizes. Some were set off by lines that made boxes. In the room surrounding him other patients read magazines. The pages had lost their gloss. The titles were so worn he couldn't read them. Each heading looked like a smudge of letters, as if someone had rubbed them while the ink was dry. These magazines hadn't been printed like that though. No one made magazines with ink that could be smudged during production anymore.

Sebastian shifted in his seat and adjusted his collar. He flipped from page to page on the clipboard. The letters on all the pages read illegibly. Maybe the copies had been bad. The ink must have smeared as the forms spat out of the machine. He looked to the receptionist who occupied himself at the computer, disinterested. The forms were indecipherable. Sebastian had the idea of the receptionist making new copies, but across the aisle the Inspector labored away with the paperwork. The other patients read the magazines with illegible titles. Were they reading or just pretending? Sebastian did not want to say anything if it was only his vision that blurred. He had had enough of being a fool in the city already. He did not put it past the Inspector to be playing a trick on him.

The sun must have beaten the sense out of him earlier in the day, he thought. Who had made a fool of him? Lack of sleep, too much heat, culture shock, jet lag — all of these could have caused the problem in his vision. But what about Julía? Had she had similar problems?

The thought was interrupted. The door off center from the reception desk, the focal point of the aisles, swung open and a man paced out, agitated. He wore a white lab coat, silver spectacles, and a shirt and tie. His body was slender, bald with tanned skin and salt and pepper hair. His steps carried him to the head of the aisle, directly before the receptionist, who looked up from the computer and tilted his head back attentively toward the newcomer. The man in the white coat addressed the crowd as a stir almost became audible.

"All of you are here to see me about the loss of people, or rather the loss of memories in people, yes?" A murmur confirmed his hypothesis. "I will address you all at once as this is the most efficient way of educating you about the occurrence. The malady has cropped up all over the city."

"I've been waiting for hours."

"All this time. I deserve a personal meeting."

"Please. Meeting with you individually wouldn't change anything I am about to say. If you are unsatisfied afterward, we can talk one to one. This is an epidemic. More doctors need to come out about this. What I tell you should be spread among you and on to others. The symptoms are … they do not vary. This is all we know about diagnosing the disease at this point in time. In some cases, partial memory returns in site-dependent episodes."

The crowd murmured, trying to comprehend.

"What?"

"If you travel to someplace that has meaning for the aggrieved, memories associated with the place may return."

"Place and memory are connected?"

"Yes. Sometimes the presence of an external factor triggers a rush of sensation unlocked by the place. A few cases had floods of memory, often uncategorized. No total recalls as of yet, but you can see why the occurrence is exciting."

A tinny voice spoke out. "What about medication?"

The only prescription available is the pneumatic Remembral. This pill only guarantees that no new memories will be lost, according to the guides. Nothing can be done about the retrieval of past memories. All other solutions will be announced as we find them."

"But that's a holistic treatment."

"It's the most effective to date. That is all."

The crowd moved in closer. The Inspector, his daughter, Sebastian, and Julía went to the stairs.

5

Sebastian and Julía went to visit the school they attended when they were young. It was in the Old Quarter with a dusty gravel yard attached to the main building. It was rare to see an open expanse in the Old Quarter and the children felt lucky to have the space in which to stretch their legs at recess.

Sebastian searched the street looking for the red and white building, the metal fence surrounding the gravel playground. His ears sought out the cries of children chasing balls kicked outside their circles, of bells calling them back to class, but he found none of it.

Where his school should have been, a set of luxury lofts was being built. The gravelly dust from the playground was now covered by the beginnings of an entrance to a parking garage on the lower levels. Shiny glass windows comprised most of the surrounding buildings façades. The modern architecture stood at odds with the older buildings in the area.

He tried to remember the days they had spent in the playground after school closed but the memories were difficult to emerge without any visual prompt. He had to rely on his experiences most of which were more than a decade old.

He wondered if that part of him was lost. If he could not remember his childhood days, did it still exist to him? Was there any importance in those past events to who he was today, or was he free to recreate himself?

Now he stood looking over an empty lot. The earth would be parted and moved aside for something new. He didn't know why he had wanted so much to escape. He should have stayed. He should have faced everything.

What had he lost in the process? Julía stood next to him, kicking stones in the dirt.

He decided to try and jog her memory. "Do you remember when my mother brought us to school? She did it in the morning, picking you up along the way."

"That never happened."

"Of course it did. We were children the last time she did it, before she died. It was your birthday."

"Your memory … the school, your mother's death. It never happened."

"You're delusional. She had just walked me to the fence. I had a gift for you. You stood on the gravel on the other side. Everyone saw. People knew about this. I remember."

"How do you know it's real, the memory?"

He wrapped his fingers around the chain link of the fence. The metal flexed slightly under his grasp. At the connecting metal post the wire rang out with the movement. The tinning sound carried over the lot. He heard it as the death knell of a memory. The school existed now only in memory. No external place could evoke the time the two had there any more. He had to find it in the files of his head and pull it forth to see under the light whenever he wanted it. He wasn't sure he even wanted it anymore. His fingers grew white over the wire links before releasing the metal. Sebastian turned to Julía. She pushed numbers on her phone, her ear bent down to hear the keys.

"Why didn't you tell me the school was gone? We could have gone someplace else."

"What?"

He placed his hands in his pockets. "I forgot. You don't know anything. What are you doing?"

"I'm making a song."

Sebastian listened to the tune she made pressing keys on her phone. He looked up to the wall across the street. Someone had drawn a face with its tongue out. He walked over to inspect it. His finger traced the lines. Coarse dust fell from his hand. Red came off on his skin.

"Lipstick? Did you …?"

A black case glittered in the sun next to her. Gold trim caught the sun as she typed on her phone. Further along a teenage boy spray painted the wall.

Sebastian walked toward the boy. His mother died in that direction. He saw himself walking there. He rounded one corner then followed the crook in the street toward the main avenue where she stepped into traffic. He could see the cars and vans buzzing past. The confines of the narrow street felt so much safer. No cars drove on them. Occasionally, you would see one pulled off to the side to deliver groceries to someone's house. The car would take up the whole street.

He kept walking through the meandering network of streets. His feet carried him like a zombie, lost in thought of the past. He plodded forward, not wanting to leave, feeling safe with old buildings creeping overhead. The din of traffic frightened him. The open expanse allowed vehicles to move at a speed much more dangerous to pedestrians. Still, he saw them mill past on the sidewalk. He didn't want to leave, but he couldn't stop walking. He saw himself stepping forward into traffic. He knew it was coming and couldn't do anything about it. This was what his mind's eye saw and still his steps carried him forward. His shoes entered the precipice where pedestrians flowed past at an angle to them. He meant to cross their river. He would thread this chaotic world.

Julía grabbed his hand. She drew him back gently and patted his shoulder. "You should watch where you're going. You have no idea where you'll end up."

As he stood blinking at the traffic, he knew something had completed within him. The drive he had away from this city no longer existed. A curious sensation ran through him. To describe it was to describe an unlocking. Numerous doors within him creaked open from his ankles through the veins in his thighs and chest on to the joints in his shoulder and wrists, even up the vertebrae of his spine. Sebastian adjusted the frame of his body to test the new acumen he found within. Everything flowed. He felt more limber. His sight seemed more vivid as well.

All of his memories had no meaning for him any more. They were lighter, unchained dreams of the past. Now he could navigate them with impunity. A long chapter of his life had closed, leaving him free to combine the elements of life as he saw fit.

Julía shifted next to him. She pulled her phone from her purse. He still wondered at her. How much of her remained? He guessed at whether there was any semblance of the person he loved left or whether she was someone different, someone new entirely. There was the sphinx of his father too nipping at his thoughts. This city no longer intimidated him though. The sphinx seemed so small in his mind. He felt as if he could unlock the mystery of the pyramids by placing his palm atop one. Such was the liberation he felt by the unlocking.

He sought for the memory of his mother, so entrenched in this place and found it dissipating. Regret filled him. He mentally retraced the corners nearby, seeking the memory of her smelling gardenias after a rainstorm; but they proved elusive, just as those memories of the past floating up into the air. These too had been unlocked. He couldn't harbor any ill will toward his father any longer. If everything else were to become free, this too had to pass.

The city was becoming a place without a history for him. He was creating everything he knew about the place as he walked. He was a man existing in the present, not the past any longer. Strange to be so free in a place that had held him back for so long. Julía had her head tilted up as if to savor the taste of blue in the sky.

He had to see Xavi. Xavi must know what happened in the city. He would have the answers Sebastian sought.

They went to the train station to catch a line heading toward the Expansion. An old bullfighting arena stood near the center of the place. He thought it an appropriate monument for the new life of the district. Taming bulls with a sword. Could businessmen be the new matador's? Hemingway wouldn't think so.

The station existed beneath a major placa in the city, the Placa Ciudad. In addition to the metro, several regional lines used this hub as a terminus for travel up and down the coast. Travel over the hills was less frequent, but if you wanted to go anywhere in the region by train, the Placa Ciudad was the place to start.

So much of his past he wanted to erase. He spent years avoiding the memories he had. He fled across an ocean, far from anyone he knew so that he could escape anything that might make him feel something, anything that might prevent him from becoming something else entirely. Still, he ended up like his father. Some things he could not change. Maybe he was wired that way.

Sebastian realized that he felt happy to have left the old man behind. No guilt clung to him. He felt liberated more so than he had in a long while. Even abroad he knew the man still existed. Some part of him dreaded sharing a world in which they both breathed. Now he was almost forgotten. Something stirred inside him and he realized he moved more lightly. As he danced, his limbs felt weightless. He could go all night if he wanted. The roof looked to have more color. The reds and blues and oranges of the sunset appeared more vivid than he had ever seen. The smell of eucalyptus wafted over from an adjoining roof. It mingled with the scent of cooking meat on a grill. He flexed his hands and felt blood coursing through his body. The sensation was dangerous. It had an addictive quality to it that made him crave more. He couldn't go back. Life was too exciting.

He wondered who cared about the people going missing in the city. Did they all learn to live without them? Were they all so crucial to the human experience that it could not be lived? He thought about these things as he moved with Opal. It was probably all misunderstandings. They could be leaving far better lives, lives someplace else. At the train station they watched people coming and going, making up stories for each person who passed. Many walked intent on their destinations in neat brisk lines. Others sat and waited patiently as the trains came late. The smell of tobacco smoke lingered in the corners of the vast station. Marble floors and pillars kept the place cool. Sebastian leaned back on a wooden bench and inhaled deeply, trying to experience the whole scene. He had felt this sensation once before, when he left. He remembered the lightness he felt, as if he could now move with more ease. Nothing held him. He did not look around save to study that which seemed interesting and new to him. He noticed children playing while their mothers knitted and waited for trains. The businessmen who tapped their feet, humming slightly as they sipped espresso in the station café. The fronds of plants turning toward the light as it moved in bolts across the floor from large rectangular windows that stood ten meters tall, the height of the station. The windows provided such warm light in the cold marble expanse. They looked out onto the world from a place where people came and went, arriving and departing from one singular point in the world. No one would be the same after passing through. They all morphed into new creatures as they underwent chemical changes — the coffee, the tobacco, the onset of puberty, old age, the sight of a new place, a new landscape — it all changed them irrevocably. Sebastian wondered at how anyone could claim they were the same person after experiencing so much and in that moment he knew how Julía felt, even if just for a moment. He looked at her, sitting next to him. She rose and tugged his sleeve hurrying off to the metro below the train station. She darted off into a car and ran out a few doors down. He trotted along, laughing at her game. She swung on poles, smiled at children, made faces through the windows, and eventually stopped.

He weathered waves of travelers. He bobbed and sidestepped through their rush, his feet tapping the marble floor of the station. These were not the actions of the Sebastian he had been when he left. But he had been acting a different Sebastian of late, one of whom he was still uncertain. The world was a whirl of ideas, ones he had never thought. He teemed to hold them, to examine them and understand each and every facet.

The doors shut. Julía waved at him, smiling. The cars moved along the platform, the windows passing more quickly as Sebastian jogged after her. She disappeared along with the fading light of the train further into the tunnel. His breath caught with heat trapped underground. Just as quickly as she had come into his life a few days earlier, she vanished into the network of railways underlying the city. At any one of the junctions she could hop off and lose herself in the pulse of the streets, leaving Sebastian behind wondering at how she had for a moment brought instances of clarity to his days. He had difficulty imagining going through the streets of the city without her again.

6

On the passing trains, he saw a ghost of her face. It flitted instantly in front of him on the window panes, like a single frame of film. He thought he couldn't have seen her. His eyes were playing tricks on him in the darkness of the underground. Still, he hurried along the platform to an earlier car, peering in to see if Julía sat in any of them. He climbed in as the doors closed.

The woman who interrogated him, Julía claiming to be someone else, the bodies in the freight container — the city was rife with mysteries. Sebastian had trouble handling the events of the past few days. None of it made sense. He couldn't figure out why he had been placed at the center of events either. There was nothing he had that anyone else could want, yet these strange occurrences seemed to follow him everywhere.

He thought about the line of questioning of the woman in the apartment in the Expansion. She was overly concerned with Xavi and his business. Sebastian had an idea he thought he'd try out and took the metro toward the business district. Behind the windows of the train, he saw graffiti flitting past, and the occasional abandoned station as the cars rumbled on underneath the city.

*

The long line of supplicants in the entryway had not changed since his last visit to Xavi's office. Sebastian walked past them, beyond the receptionist who stood up protesting when he passed, and into Xavi's office.

Xavi sat behind a desk, his feet on the top with a cat's cradle of string laced between his fingers.

The receptionist followed him in. "I told him you were busy."

He raised a hand. "So what's this all about, Sebastian?"

"It was your apartment."

"What are you talking about?"

"I lost consciousness when I went to work for Grey. I woke up in someone's apartment. It was yours."

He looked to the receptionist and nodded for her to leave.

"Here, let me give you something to ease the bump on your head. You must still be suffering from your fall."

Xavi went to a cart topped with several bottles of liquor, a few cylindrical glasses that glinted in the light, and a bucket of ice. He dropped some ice cubes into a glass and made a mixture of liquor and tonic water. The concoction fizzed as he handed it to Sebastian. "Take this." The glass felt smooth in his hand. Xavi placed two white tablets in Sebastian's palm with instructions to swallow both.

Sebastian stared into his hand at the white cylindrical tablets. A line bisected the center of the pill, dividing each into two identical white semi-circles. "It was your assistant who asked me back. Why did she bring me here?"

"Not sure what you're talking about, Sebastian. But you should come with me. I have some work you might be interested in."

Sebastian meant to persist, but the cityscape beyond the windows stopped him. It had changed since the previous visit. The window behind him looked out onto the skyline of the Expansion. From his seat, one could see a dozen or so cranes at work on various buildings in the city. Sebastian did not recognize many of the structures, so quickly they were being raised. "What happened to the skyline?"

"Hm? That's what I was trying to tell you about. There's work to be done."

"It's changed in just a few days."

"You need to pay more attention. It's the sign of progress my friend. I'll show you."

∗

Xavi hailed a black and yellow Nacionale cab. Museum postcards of still lives and nudes decorated the dash and ran up the armrest of the passenger door. A few street scenes and pictures of children smiling mixed into the lot. Xavi busied himself with the cat's cradle again as they rode in the taxi.

Sebastian looked around. He had lost track of where they were. On the corner he saw some graffiti. He looked closer to examine the image. It passed too quickly but another appeared further along the street. Beyond the corner pedestrian traffic milled as usual. He pinned these tags together, connecting one to another through the streets, slowly picking his way toward something, what he did not know. One read 'React.' Another 'Rebel.' The words ran under a stencil of a three-eyed man in uniform weighing a bully club in his hand and smiling in front of a factory.

The cab driver spoke to them.

"Artists paint still lives for a reason. They were glimpses into the details of life. Some centuries old. They are the only snapshots we have of how people lived. No one notices the details now."

Along the street, a man emerged from around the corner. His pace frantic, he fled past the taxi. His eyes, wide with the terror, latched onto the sight of Sebastian. He ran up to the taxi and banged on the window. The neighborhood seemed home mostly to immigrants living in neglected buildings. Two more men emerged behind the man. They pulled the immigrant from the window and put an arm bar on each side. It was only then, when faced with his freedom, that this man knew it would never be. They ground his face against the stones. His pockets were emptied and he was pressed against the white walls disintegrating in the Old Quarter. One was holding the fugitive's face against the stone wall while the other searched him.

The two policemen carried him roughly back the way they came. He protested at first but after a jab in the stomach, hung limp. His head hung low as if his fate was sealed. The taxi lurched forward into traffic. Sebastian felt something base had changed in its character. Where would he fit within its walls now?

"You shouldn't have asked me to come back."

Xavi didn't seem to notice anything unusual happening outside the taxi. "I didn't ask you to come back. My assistant can be overzealous. If I had known she meant to interrogate you, I wouldn't have approved. She tends to act independent of me often. I'm not sure why I keep her on."

They arrived at a large construction site along a boulevard that ran parallel to the shoreline. Palms bent with the breeze on the other side of the boulevard. Two or three people on roller skates passed on the boardwalk. Aside from them, the only people to be seen were the construction workers.

Large sections of earth had been excavated to make way for the foundations of the buildings. Sebastian looked down on sloping dirt ramps that ran along the walls of the excavation. Trucks hauled out excess debris while another vehicle scraped armfuls of earth from the bottom of the site. A kind of wire netting held the walls from collapsing on the scene of work men and machines below. Large girders were being pounded into the ground as well. Sebastian heard the pile driver making contact like a gunshot's report.

Xavi walked up to the edge of the construction site. He talked looking over the site and the surrounding buildings, but not at Sebastian. "This is what I was telling you about. The area used to be industrial. That was until we bought up most of the neighborhood and cleaned it out.

That took some time. People had moved in to the abandoned warehouses and factories. They actually lived in these derelict places. These kinds of projects allow for a large profit. You can be involved too if you want. Grey asked me to show you around since things didn't work out at the other place."

"Why do you need me? First Grey wanted me, now you. I was happy to leave this city behind."

"You'd be surprised at the kinds of things we found when we dug down. Old cars, barrels of waste, even a skeleton or two. Makes you wonder what was happening here before we got involved. We had to call the Society for Historic Preservation a few times. They were up in arms about 'preserving the heritage of the city.' It didn't take much to keep them quiet though.

"People are making a killing off these projects. You can be a part of it too. We sell luxury lofts at inflated prices with high maintenance fees. That way revenue never stops. The materials are shoddy. Walls are hollow. Noise carries. Someone once told me the granite was on discount because of low radioactivity levels. There's no place else to live. We've acquired so much real estate. Even the shops on the ground level give a percentage of sales."

"I don't have anything to invest."

"That's the beauty of it. You can create the zeitgeist. We need someone to drive the price up. Once the inflated price bursts we buy everything back cheap and do the process all over again. You'll get a fractional percentage."

"I know how to build houses, not sell them."

"Well, that's the thing. We need a figurehead. If we can say that we have a Veillard as the architect, the project's worth will skyrocket."

"There are people disappearing in this city, and you want me to invest in some scam? Julía was right about you. You've sold the city out."

Xavi stepped back from the edge of the excavation site. He looked directly into Sebastian and spoke. "You still don't get it. No one here cares anymore. You're the last one making any noise. You've got to make a profit while you still can. Everyone else is already on board. They're not looking back either. Don't be left out of this. It will ruin you. You'll end up like the squatters we relocated."

Sebastian bristled. "What did you do to them? Did you ship them out like at the dock?"

Xavi returned quickly. "It's what your father was doing. He may have been stubborn, but he wasn't stupid. He saw the writing on the wall. He knew that he had to either bend his rules a little or break. So many of them break."

Sebastian wondered how the man he had feared for so long would acquiesce. He couldn't picture it. There had to be something else, something more than money. The man wouldn't have sacrificed his principles for a scam housing project. His madness had to be more than shame. Something else gripped the city, something Xavi wouldn't tell him about, but his father knew.

"You're a disgrace." Sebastian left. He needed to clear his head. He walked into the streets of the city hoping to lose himself in the winding cobbled walks he had frequented in his youth. It was a long way from the industrial section in which he stood, but he had an excess of restless energy to burn.

7

Sebastian began to see these kinds of projects all over the city. It seemed that at every corner he saw steel girders being pounded into a dugout of ground. Levels began to emerge from vertical lines of the girders as platforms were built that rose higher and higher into the sky.

They came so rapidly that Sebastian had trouble finding his way through the streets. Landmarks he once used disappeared. Instead of a quiet cathedral, a shopping mall graced the corner of a block. Crowds came with the new structures too. He had to pick his way through people toting boutique shopping bags. These crowds were loud, filled with chatter that made Sebastian yearn for a quieter walk.

Sebastian felt heady from the buzz of the crowds and the changing buildings. He found a metro entrance and descended between wrought iron gates made with artistic flourish. The heat from the sun above diminished once underground. Sebastian felt beads of sweat cooling on his forehead. He stopped to catch his breath. His chest had tightened above and he leaned back against a wall. The cold tiles soothed him. A train arrived on the track opposite the platform on which he stood. A rush of hot air blew past, giving the momentary sensation of temperate weather.

Graffiti covered the train. People's tags and murals surrounded the windows through which passengers could be seen boarding the train across the platform.

Before him broken tiles of ceramic lined the wall of the metro platform. Each tiny piece, none larger than a centimeter, had been placed by the hands of the artist into mortar. Verdant green vines twisted along the frame of the mosaic. Each strand interweaved with others in an intricate pattern knotting the scene of the gods firmly in place. An expanse of fields tilled to produce vegetation untied the two halves of the wall. On one side, Apollo in all his rigid glory stood upright. Hues of yellow, beige, and white created a subtle contrast in the rays emanating from him. Each bolt spread forth from him like the shot of an arrow. The fields before him grew grain tilled by farmers, some looking to him for advice. His stolid eyes unmoving, stared across toward the other end of the tiles. The golden grains changed, tile by tile, to a burnt red earth. In the blushing soil, half clothed people slept. The furrows in the earth produced vines laden heavy with grapes. Some plucked the fruit, placing handfuls in their cheeks. The deep purple made their faces rosy. The tiles surrounding the scene no longer bore the same light sandy hue as Apollo's side. Darkness spread from purple to black shadow. In it, the occasional white robe lay discarded on the ground. Deep in the cracked tiles of midnight blue, purple, and black sat Dionysus. The mischievous grin that gave birth to bacchanals gleamed white. He seemingly grinned at Apollo, delighting in his followers who cavorted around him. The contrast from purple and blue tiles dotting the shadow looked as if notes of music were strewn from a harp nearby. Across the expanse of countryside, these two gods stared at one another, locked in eternal contrast as a tile relief of the vigor characterizing two extremes of humankind. Someone had spray painted the word *West* over the mosaic in large letters that dripped due to a heavy application. The stem of the 'T' shot downward then turned at an angle toward Apollo and pointed to the darkness of the tracks leading away into the metro tunnel.

West. The word was everywhere. He remembered the scene at the police station. Julia knew something about this as well. Her transformation into Opal had been so sudden. Now, in her wake he stared face to face with the mystery of his father again. Why did she hide from him then?

Just as he came to reacquaint himself with the unfamiliar environs of the city, this word drew him back to the disappearance of his father. All the inertia created from Julía in the past few days dwindled to a stop before the graffiti. The catch of his breath — that heady warmth of excitement that made him forget, allowing him to live — dissipated like the vibrations of the train as it passed further along the tracks. The hum still rang in his ears, but as a ghost of something lost. Now he stood facing the memory of the man who brought him back. A clawing sensation overcame him, one that constricts the limbs and makes people clench their teeth and hands. He had to go on. The only defense he had against the sensation was to go on. Sebastian followed the bright, fluid letters along the train to the end of the platform. The word *West* was spray-painted onto the wall in bold block letters. He drew nearer. The stem of the 'T' pointed down, toward the train tracks in a jagged arrow leading the way. Sebastian looked back at his platform. No one paid any attention. The metro workers yawned in the heat. Passengers waited for the train. Some smoked. Some chatted idly. Sebastian waited for the next train to come. A rush of people came out of the cars and headed toward the streets above. The train left and Sebastian lowered himself onto the tracks following the direction of the 'T' in *West*. The eyes of a small boy being tugged along by his mother lingered on Sebastian's form as it disappeared in the darkness.

8

He had to see how his father disappeared in the city. Maybe by knowing what drove the man mad he could control the encroaching feeling of absence the city produced. The sensation differed from other absences, ones that brought glints of freedom to the mind.

In the tunnel, light came sporadically. Passing trains shook the ground on which he walked and startled him with glimpses into the light of passing cars. Each time his eyes had to adjust to the darkness, momentarily dilated by the world of train passengers. The irises would become accustomed to the dark and he could make out rats scurrying along the rails, and steel girders supporting the tunnel. When trains from behind rumbled in the distance, he ducked into recesses along the walls.

He could see trains running by on parallel tracks thirty meters out. The tracks split into a Y, down one arm of which a ghost station stood forgotten. The tile work cracked over decades of neglect. An old train car had been parked at the station next to a wedge shaped platform. In and around the car, Sebastian saw lights and shadowy forms moving. A few men in their twenties and teenagers milled about the metro tunnel. The sound of wheels on cement filled the tunnel. Sebastian heard the click clack of skateboards and a hiss of spray paint as it marked the walls. One skater noticed Sebastian and approached him. His hair was shaved on each side. Long natty dreads fell from the back of his head, though the top looked a muffled black mess. The young man took a few tugs on a spliff and offered it to Sebastian.

Sebastian declined.

"You don't smoke? Then what are you doing down here?"

"Yeah, what are you doing down here?" another asked.

A circle began to form around Sebastian. He could not see all of their faces. Most were backlit. Dirt smeared the few that he did see. An occasional glint of light reflected off what Sebastian thought must be facial piercings.

"You don't belong here."

"This place is ours."

"Ours, not yours."

A sense of menace overcame Sebastian as he was physically cordoned off amid the group. There was no one to protect him down here. No one even knew where he was. He had to think. He had to act quickly. He had followed the word *West* here. He had to know if there was a connection between his father and these men.

They had painted all kinds of symbols on the walls. Anarchy symbols with the A and a circle around it, aliens and pyramids, skeletons. Names too. *West* was written on the outside of the car as well.

Sebastian pointed to *West*. "That symbol. Who made it?"

"Wouldn't you like to know?"

Another felt the fabric of his shirt. "Why should we tell you?"

"I saw that symbol when the city police station was attacked. It's all over the walls of my house too. My father, he disappeared."

"You hear that? His father disappeared."

"Not the first one."

"What are you going to cry about it?"

They came closer. A hand reached out and pushed him back by the shoulder. He had to stand his ground. There was no turning back.

"Maybe Pavel did it. Hey, Pavel."

A lanky, pale skinned man rose up from the base of the wall where he sat. He had a shaved head with bristles of blond hair sticking out from his temples and brow.

"Pavel, man. What's that?"

Pavel took a drag from the spliff. He did a French exhale, blowing it out his mouth while inhaling it back into his nose. Bloodshot eyes, his lids drooping so that he could barely see, he spoke in a low monotone. "You don't want to know. Go back where you came from."

"You're the only people in this city who seem to have any idea who he is. These words led me here. One of you has to know."

The man laughed, open mouthed, and ribbed Pavel. "We all share here. What's mine is yours. What's Rodrigo's is mine, and so on. What do you have to offer?"

"You live here?"

"We're squatting on this place."

"Why?"

"There are no cameras down here. We can live as we want. We can be free."

"There are cameras above?"

"Haven't you read Orwell? They're fucking everywhere. Here we're free."

"You don't need electricity? Water?"

"Man, we can find that anywhere. That's what fountains are for. This is a place to sleep and have fun. Go check in the car. Maybe Rodrigo will help you."

Small clusters sat cross-legged in groups, smoking and passing bottles between them along the station wall. They were silhouetted by the lights hooked up to a generator. Every so often the glint of a bottle reflected the floodlights. Stairs at the broad end of the platform led up then split to go both left and right. Tile letterwork at the top read Estació Hôpital though many of the tiles were chipped or had fallen out. He heard music. Someone played a guitar in the car.

Sebastian followed the rails up to the car, walked around the side, where the doors were open and called in. He heaved himself into the car, placing both hands at the entrance to the door and pushed himself up.

Some of the seats had been removed from the car. Cots and sleeping bags lined the open sections along with jugs of water, canned goods and clothes bundled up.

"West. The symbol outside. What does it mean?"

"He's crazy. Look at him. He's crazy."

"The sign, it led me here. Why did you paint it?"

The one called Rodrigo shook the can of spray paint. The hiss from the depressed nozzle filled the abandoned car. Sebastian turned to see Rodrigo covering the windows with paint. No one could see in or out the panes he covered. He sprayed one after another until one end of the car blacked out.

"Why does anyone do anything?" Rodrigo said over his shoulder. "Because we want to." He continued to paint the remaining windows. Light from the portable lamps stayed outside the metal of the car. Only the glow from their flashlights and spliffs lit the inside of the abandoned vehicle.

"I've seen it before, in a journal. The author wrote it everywhere. Tell me what it means."

Their leader tugged on a spliff. "And if we don't? You going to make us tell you?" The group sitting in a circle laughed.

Rodrigo turned. "Yeah, what are you going to do?"

"It's the only clue I have. The author, he's gone missing. I don't know what else to do."

The leader weighed Sebastian's speech. "Rodrigo, you hear that? The man's gone missing."

The hissing stopped. "Everyone's gone. My sister, my little sister left too. It's sad." He threw the can of spray paint on the floor. It rattled as it rolled.

Cesar continued. "We're at war. None of us asked for it but we've been pushed so far aside that there's no place else for us to go. Look at us. We even live underground. I can't stand by and watch as we're oppressed, bled for every cent we have. There's life in us. I'll be damned if I'll let some corporate thugs take that away from me. That's all the police are. Follow the money. They obey whoever pays them. The state, too, they bow to special interests. All you have to do is pay for the campaign and you get your legislation made for you. The government looks the other way when its time for you to pay taxes. Meanwhile, we live down here, like dogs.

"Some people feel like we do. Even within the system, we have sympathizers. No one wants to be a cog forever. Especially when there's no escape, no end in sight. It's our very lives we're fighting for. I can't think of any more noble fight than the one for our freedom. We can't let them take that from us."

A chorus of approvals erupted from the group. Sebastian stood in the midst of revolutionaries. He wondered at what cost their equality would come. How much of the society he knew would be sacrificed in the name of freedom. It's one thing to address repression, but you must replace one structure with another. He doubted they had a plan to support the city. They were a band of outcasts seeking personal liberty more than anything else. How could his father have become mixed up with them?

"West. What does it mean?"

"You're a particular one. It's become a sort of a rallying call, but we never made it up. The word just started appearing all over the city. It showed up wherever we were. Pavel knows where it first started."

Pavel was the pink skinned man with a shaved head. He stood up and went to the doors of the car. "I'll show you." He jumped out the open doors into the tunnel.

They climbed the stairs at the broad end of the wedge platform leading up under Estació Hôpital. They walked the ghost station's upper platform. The sound of the skateboard wheels resembled thunder as it resounded against the underground walls. He took one last glance at the okupas and ventured onward into the side tunnel. The floodlights faded in this area.

From Pavel's flashlight Sebastian could see *West* written over the walls.

"This guy's has been tagging everything. It's all he does. Even things that aren't nailed down. Buses, trains. I saw a dog once."

Pavel slid a heavy cargo door on a track with a wheel for a locking mechanism.

"In here." He flicked a switch on the wall a few times. Nothing happened. Rodrigo cursed. "The fuses in this place are old. This happens sometimes. Not to worry. Wait here. I'll go change them."

He slid the door closed behind Sebastian. The lurching sound of the door resting into its final place had an air of finality to it.

"What are you doing?"

"It's so you don't get lost. I won't be long."

Panic seized Sebastian's breathing. His chest tightened. He wondered how he could be so stupid as to be trapped by these squatters. His mind ran through a series of scenarios in which they would try to ransom him, rob him, then, finding he had no money, harvest him for organs.

Sebastian regretted following the sign down the tracks. He did not know why he obeyed such a random sign. Julía had left on the train and there it was: *West*, pointing the way forward. He had no other ideas at the time save for this mantra, written over the words of his father's manuscript. Sebastian wished he could be rid of it. The whole scene was a mess he never wanted and it became messier by the minute. Julía, or Opal as she called herself earlier that day, mystified him. She pretended to have no memory of him, not a whit of her cells devoted in her brain to recognizing his face. Sebastian deserved worse for abandoning her all those years ago, but he kept asking himself why she was drawn to him? Maybe he kept some key to the past that unlocked parts of her personality she had forgotten years ago; but if that were the case why pretend? He should have followed her. He should have boarded the train. Then he could find answers to one of the mysteries populating his life in the city.

He used the light from his phone to look around the room.

The tunnel resembled a cell in that the walkway became a cul-de-sac with a heavy iron door that swung creakily closed after he entered. Iron bars allowed a view into the main tunnel of the catacomb where Rodrigo and the other squatters discussed what to do with Sebastian. Sebastian tried calling out to them a few times but they ignored his voice. The space looked lighter outside, outside the bars, where fluorescent movable lamps jerry rigged to a humming generator illuminated the underground passage.

Inside the cul-de-sac Sebastian saw brick and mortar walls on either side capped by a rounded ceiling. At the end, more of the same. The scene reminded him of The Cask of Amontillado, save he had no wine and he was likely the person to be walled in. A small stream of runoff slid under the door along the concave bottom of the cul-de-sac. The stream emptied into a grate built into the floor where it joined the end wall. Next to the grate Sebastian made out a pile of clothes; at least that's what he thought, at first. The pile shuffled and he realized it was another person. The person sat up in grayish rags stained with brown all over. He wore a beard, long and grey, a similar color to his clothes, and had hair down past his shoulders. He looked as if he could have been in the cell for months. The thought of it frightened Sebastian.

Pavel returned with a woman. "The sign on the metro platform? My sister Mizu tagged it. It's become kind of a rallying call. Won't tell anyone what it means either. She's in and out like that. Not conscious like the rest of us. Even me, her own brother only gets small phrases of information.

"There are others. They seem to know about it too, but none of them talk much. We stand up for them. They're why we act. No one wants to end up empty. They don't even know they're lost.

"She thinks cell phones brainwashed people to forget. I think it's the internet. They catch everything.

"*West* is an arts collective. Mizu is a part of it. They all take turns blowing up walls with murals, tags, community — any kind of visual. They all say something. Most of them are wiped like Mizu. When they start spraying though, something comes out. They're different. You can see something take over. They're not their old selves. It's like a trance. The art guides them.

"It's all connected somehow too. They seem to have the same message. No idea how it's done, but once they start painting it's another world for them. It's the only way you can get them to be active. Otherwise they're like vegetables — zombies just walking around without noticing anything. I waved my hands in front of her between trances and she didn't even register it. When they're painting it's the same, but you get the feeling they can see through you. Gives me the creeps. But what am I going to do? She's my sister. I have to take care of her.

"Mizu says it's because the cell phones brainwashed them. She told me in between vegetative states. Just kind of stared at the wall and spoke to no one in particular. I just happened to be there. No idea what she says when no one is around. She thinks it was in the tubes. Made her change her name. She doesn't respond to her given name."

"She took on a new name?"

"Yeah. Weird. I got used to it after a while, but she was a blank slate for a while. Wiped clean. When she came out of it she was part of this collective. It's like they know already, like they're in a cocoon or something gestating. Mizu began to connect. Some of the old Kristina was in, but distant, like speaking through a tunnel.

"Anyway, the art collective throws up work wherever they can. It's become a call for anyone who has lost someone. We all get it when we see they're art, not the meaning they intend, but the loss of someone who now creates the stuff. Their work is a door to another world. When you see it, people like us aren't far behind. You've already found one easter egg. Others are all over the city. She doesn't use phones now too."

"I don't mind phones," said Mizu, speaking for the first time.

"Right. She doesn't like to use them, I guess."

"You just have to recognize what they are. Some things are more real than others."

She borrowed Pavel's phone and dialed an assortment of number combinations — none of which could have been someone's number — and spoke words in sequence. "Un. Deux. Trois. Canary red. Chicks Yellow. Mushroom pizza spoor. Delivery. Train. Delivery. Transit. Network fare. Farewell. Well. Bats. Bout Mahler. Bird. Wind-up. Clock. Praha."

Sebastian noticed they were word associations. Her meaning was hidden somewhere in the code. He couldn't unlock it though.

"Their speech. Why do they talk like that?"

"I don't know. It's unnerving, but you get used to it. Come on. I'll show you the way out."

9

He began to disbelieve everything he saw. Julía's double. Mizu. The underground scene. He had difficulty believing it. The experience seemed so real. The viscera of the scene in the metro underground still felt fresh in his senses. Mizu knew things, too, about what happened in the city. Perhaps it was an external representation of what he already knew. There had been much to process since his return. His mind could have worked itself into a frenzy and illuminated those connections he had not been able to consciously make. He went through explanations for the experience. Darkness plays tricks on the mind. The sound of a rat could be someone clawing. As your irises adjust, the darkness loses shape. Individual forms begin to emerge. The mind attempts to match images with what is known to exist. Sometimes these conclusions can be wrong. If you've never seen a shape before, how can you recognize it? The familiar will appear out of the dark before the unknown. The mind sees what it wants to see. The rumble of the metro continued.

He kept coming back to what Xavi's assistant wanted. Julía had made him forget about it but the two were connected — Julía becoming Opal and people going missing — they were part of the same phenomena gripping the city. His father did not have a unique fate. He was one of many. The old man would not be happy to see that his life was not so different from the others. Maybe he knew, Sebastian thought. The tide of missing people could be part of what he was onto. It could be the thing that drove him mad. Sebastian tried to imagine how he would react if he learned that an epidemic broke out in the city. The man had cared so much for the city, for Sebastian to the point of strangling him out of it. An epidemic of missing people, of changing houses, of a city skyline that morphed overnight; these were the things the man had been contemplating.

Sebastian could not trust the accounts he had from Grey and Xavi. They were too suspect to have provided him with a real glimpse of what happened. There was too much to hide. His father had known, but with that knowledge what would he have done? There was an artifice behind the experiences he had so far in the city. People lied their way through the days. For a moment, he wondered if he should leave it all behind, as he had before. The intrigue was too pressing. If an entire city lost all recollection of who they were, there would be no boundaries for what one could do. Anyone could take control and mold the place to suit whatever plans they made. He didn't like the thought of the city being shaped like that.

*

At the address Xavi's assistant had given him was a shop selling textiles. Inside, rugs covered the floor from wall to wall, with piles of the carpets nestled against the wall. A man sat on one of the piles near the floor smoking a hookah. He raised his eyebrows slowly and looked sideways at Sebastian. As he exhaled, another man parted the beads hanging from the back of the store and went to the counter in the rear. He was an exact double of the man smoking.

"Can we help you?" the one behind the counter asked.

"You have something of mine."

"What's that?"

Sebastian was at an impasse. He didn't know exactly what he was to get.

"I was sent to pick something up."

The man sitting down spoke. "Join me." Sebastian sat down. "Here." The man handed him a hose. Sebastian took a pull off the hookah. "What he's looking for is down below."

"Down below? I see."

The man smoking talked. "There is no work. The only jobs are on those stupid deconstruction projects. What are they doing anyway? Why build something just to take it down? It's madness.

"One percent equals one hundred percent. It's whole, you see. From one decimal column to the next. One is a hundred percent of one unit. Binary code is like that. You either get it or you don't. Ones and zeroes. Being and nothingness. In one point all others exist. There are different scales of the infinite."

Sebastian's head felt dizzy. His eyesight clouded at the glint of sun coming through the window. "What about the ninety-nine? Are they ninety-nine wholes?"

"You don't get it, do you? He wouldn't. He doesn't know."

"Know what?" asked Sebastian.

They paused to confirm something between each other with a nod. "We've seen the aleph. It showed us what a whole is. And isn't. You don't know, so you don't believe."

Sebastian looked at him, dumbfounded. "Alephs don't exist. It's a myth for mystics. They use it to swindle people."

The smoker grasped Sebastian by the hand. "Alephs are real. They contain multitudes. Either you believe or you don't. There is work either way."

"It's not about work," said Sebastian.

"You're right. He's right. Alephs are a beginning. Once you see it, you'll understand. Come. We'll have to show him."

The man behind the counter wrinkled his nose. He walked in front of Sebastian and rolled back the carpet to show a hatch underneath. It lifted up revealing a ladder below. The smoker told him to go.

An identical twin of the smoker waited at the foot of the ladder. "Sebastian. The uninitiated. It's good to see you. There's an aleph here. You should have a look for yourself. Feel it's power. Once you see it you'll understand."

They descended. The twin from behind the counter was reunited with his brother. Below were stucco walls and wine racks. Cots and dirty clothes lined many parts of the floor. They stepped through the patchwork of debris toward a chamber further within. A few people sat between the racks. Their arms encircled their knees and they shook constantly. They looked at the visitors anxiously.

The twin withdrew a bottle and reached into the rack. He pulled his arm out and handed Sebastian a small flash drive.

"Is this what I'm here for?"

"This is one half. You don't get it do you?" The smoker's twin continued. "You can't see what happens to them? I had you all wrong. The buildings have collected energy over time. The lives of the people who inhabit them radiate energy. It builds up in the woodwork and frames. Over time it reaches a breaking point. The energy has to be released. Otherwise the house's energy becomes off. That's what hauntings are — malcontent energy radiated from previous lives."

"This city is so old. There are so many buildings coursing with energy. I've found a way to collect the energy of those radiated souls. Even the houses have an energy all their own. Once we harness the energy collected, we can trade it on the energy market like any other product."

"Dead souls. Gogol tried that."

"Yes, but he never believed in the energy of the soul. Just like Grey. All he sees is the money to be gained. I thought you understood the potential of energy. You've seen him looking for the aleph, haven't you?"

"How could you know anything about my father?"

"I helped people look for it. Xavi too for a while, but he gave up on its existence. You can still help. You have that sense about you. I know you can feel the aleph in this world.

"This and other places allow us a glimpse into the world of what will be. They're portals to the rest of the world. We can't step through them, but the light is ancient. The light travels not through space but through a fold in the world. The city is rich with them. That's why we're really digging. We're searching for alephs. You'd be a great help with your sensory faculties attuned to portals like this."

Sebastian looked at the pillar. It stood in the center of the room flecked with color. The more he looked at it the less he saw of the surrounding room. It drew into the background and the flecks of the pillar filled his vision. As he stared these flecks began to dance. They moved about like jumping beans until something changed. The depth of the pillar was no longer flat. The flecks stood in the foreground and the marble became a three-dimensional space. He stared into it, looking through the pillar until he saw a table and some chairs. The vision became stronger. More tables emerged at the edges of his vision. They were silver and people dined at the table. It was the Placa Ciudad. His view must have been from one of the lampposts at the center by the fountain.

"These are what we're really looking for when we excavate the grounds."

Sebastian stepped back from the portal. He felt as if his eyes had crossed and latched onto their lines of sight. A minute or two passed as his vision came back to the normal lighting in the cellar. "You can see them, see through space."

"They're very powerful. You have no idea of the energy that can be harvested through them. I'm collecting the souls of these houses with the use of alephs. Once we have enough we can channel them into new buildings. It's like feng shui. Buildings have souls. The have to be oriented in a certain way to align with the environment. Otherwise, the spirits of the surrounding area become angry. The last thing we want in an expanding city is the spirits of ancestors raising havoc. It won't do for solid growth. Your father knew this, that buildings have souls. He knew about the alephs too, but could never find one. This one was only uncovered recently. His belief in alephs is ultimately why he decided to help us. He wanted to keep the spirits at peace. I'm collecting the souls to keep the new growth from being haunted."

"But what about the old ones? What do you do with them?"

The twin hesitated, "There's a way of harnessing them. I'm sure of it. We can use their energy. You wouldn't understand. I'm just now starting my research on this unearthed aleph. It's arcane work not suited to an architect like you."

*

Sebastian took the Promenade on the way back and watched the buskers performing for the crowds. His head spun. Something in the hookah got to him. The buskers stood still as statues only to become animated when someone placed a few coins in front of them. He found himself staring at their costumes. Their stillness unnerved him. The smoker must have been lying to him. Alephs don't exist. It had to be a trick. No one would deconstruct a city looking for some mythical source of energy. The busker moved and Sebastian became startled. He moved away and backed into another busker behind him.

He decided he should see Xavi and ask him about the process. Xavi was up to his ears in the mess of the city. He would clear things up for Sebastian. Life in the streets was too confusing for Sebastian after the hookah.

*

Xavi's assistant met him at the entryway.

"What's taken you so long? I haven't seen Xavi for days. Something's not right."

Sebastian held out the flash drive for her. "They showed me an aleph. Alephs don't exist, right? They can't be real. He said this would help me understand."

"Please, calm down. This isn't a conversation we should have in front of other people." She ushered him back from the rows of people waiting to see him. She closed the door behind him and spoke to Sebastian.

"He told you about alephs, right? They drugged you. The tea was drugged. Alephs don't exist. It's just some myth Arturo tells people to get them in line. Having some supernatural initiation helps in controlling people's minds, doesn't it?"

How could he believe her? The vision had been so real, from one place to another.

"Let's see what you found." She connected the drive to her computer and opened the only file on it. A video appeared. Xavi sat on a couch. Dim light emanated at a slant from a conical lamp shade. His face dipped in and out of the light as he talked. Xavi's eyes appeared less frequently. When they did, the eyes looked made, fraught. He clasped his hair with both hands running back from his forehead before releasing his grip. Air met his empty fingers and he continued his rant.

"It took me hours to accept that I had to record this video. It was the only way out. You'll see. They know about you. You can't stop them. I tried. How do you think I ended up in this situation, in the exact situation you are in right now? Progress must be made. Stand against it and you'll break. My god, they all break. I tried to play but look at me. Look at me. Dammit." He sobbed. "You'll see Sebastian. They're coming to you. For what it's worth, I'm sorry you had to learn about it like this."

"All the men in my office, their lives have been taken. Their houses bought, their families disappeared, they have nothing. They are left to begging for their lives back. Even if they make an agreement they have lives of servitude ahead. They're really better off waiting. I doubt they even know why they're here.

"Julía too. She was almost out. I'm not sure what happened with her. I was too busy looking after myself. Now she remembers nothing. She's not the first either. This is the epidemic. People are losing themselves.

"They're watching you. Following you too, most likely. Some of them in the lobby are probably spies. I only had time to record this before I left the city. I can't trust people in the office. There are too many people involved for me to single out one person. I felt I had to do something for you, though. Your father would have expected that. There's so much that you need to know. This epidemic, people disappearing, it's engineered. They want people to forget. If the city forgets, they can do anything. Don't let them do the same to you. Get out before you're trapped. Leave the site. Leave your father. Just go. You did it before quite well."

When the video ended, a live feed of Sebastian replaced the window. The camera on the computer showed Sebastian's puzzled face.

"This isn't right. It was supposed to be for him, not you. What did you do?"

Sebastian closed the open window on the computer. "This is what they gave me."

"They had evidence. That's why he worked for them. How could he have left without me? Why didn't he leave something for me?"

Sebastian thought of what happened to Xavi after he left the other night. He hadn't trusted him. Xavi knew all along of what transpired in the city but hid it from Sebastian. Why hadn't he told him earlier?

He decided to check one of the things Xavi said. Sebastian went to the entryway and talked to one of the men waiting.

"Why are you here?"

"I'd like to have my life back."

"What does your house look like?"

"Eh?"

"Your house, what does it look like?"

The man looked puzzled, as if sorting through the overstuffed drawers of memory for a missing sock. "I ... I don't know."

"How long have you been here?"

"I can't remember. I've been here as long as I can tell."

"No one remembers what the land looks like. The land, it's forgotten. There's no place else?"

"Well, I can picture other places, though I don't think I've been to them."

"Unbelievable. And you?"

"The same, sir."

"This is what Xavi has been doing. These people, he created them."

Xavi's assistant took a step back. "Strange. He'd never do that."

Sebastian thought about his father and the double he found under the city.

"All the men are here for their houses, yet none remember what they look like and he's telling me to protect mine? Why did he do this?"

"How could he?"

Sebastian took the papers and threw them at the lines of men waiting as he walked out the entranceway. If these men were as lost as Julía, the epidemic could cover the whole city.

10

There was no biological explanation for it. Losing one's memory, one's sense of place and self, it couldn't biologically happen. A widespread occurrence of so many different cases suggested that it would be contagious, viral even, yet Sebastian had not contracted a seizing case of amnesia. There must be some kind of eternal factor causing psychological loss in the city's inhabitants. Grey had something to do with this impetus. He had to. He was at the center of it all.

Along the way they had lost something. A sense of place, perhaps. There was no sense of wonder at the world, at the marvel of actually existing. It was all taken for granted, as if the luxuries of food out of season and electricity were their birthrights. Sebastian knew what this meant. He had struggled on his own. He had known hunger. He had lived in shacks without running water. He had come to appreciate how infinitesimal he was compared to this vast universe. The fact that he existed, he thought, felt passion, made him respect the everyday. Instead of appreciating the marvel of their modern world, the people he saw inhabiting worlds like Xavi's were spiritually dead. He wondered what had become of the city to see so many defined by what they consumed. Before he became lost in this world, Sebastian needed to act.

He shook with each small bounce, steeling his nerves for what would be an unpleasant visit. If Xavi wasn't home, he would search the apartment for clues about what was happening in this city. His head still felt clouded by his visit to the supposed aleph.

*

Xavi's apartment was the same place Sebastian had first been interrogated. Sebastian looked over the place with a head that was not groggy this time. Xavi paced back and forth, chain smoking. The blood in Sebastian's head became tense. Sounds seemed amplified. Xavi looked for the entrance, wandering around the room like a madman.

The skyline had changed again. All the buildings that obstructed the ones Sebastian knew were now being disassembled. A crane's arm drew materials from the top of one of these skyscrapers. Sebastian suppressed a small shiver at seeing this.

Xavi seemed affected too. He placed one hand on a white wall and his arm slid down as his legs buckled. Sebastian held him up as his arm knocked over a crystal vase that spilled water and debris from cut plants onto the floor. Sebastian drew him into the corridor where he pressed the button for the elevator.

"What have you done?"

"I was trying to help. Do what you want. You always have."

The bell dinged. Xavi and Sebastian entered the elevator and Sebastian pressed the button for him. "I hope you find what you're looking for. I really do." Xavi tried a diffident smile as the doors shut. "We have to go. I'm on my way out. Come with me. We can talk there."

"Where are you going?"

"I need to get to my boat. It's important I arrive soon."

"Fine."

"There's so much you don't know, Sebastian. I wanted something better for you, but you couldn't wait around for it."

A black sedan pulled up in front of them. The driver unrolled the window. The passenger door opened and a large man in a suit stepped out toward them. "Grey sent us for you. Please get in."

He rode in silence, so furious he was at Xavi for taking part in this mess. Xavi had been lying to him. There was nothing left of his old friend. The man had been replaced by opportunism running rampant in the city. The housing affair vexed Sebastian more. Why would someone buy all the houses in the city? Why did they all want the houses back, if they ever existed in the first place? Sebastian wondered what it was they lost in their deals. Xavi must have misled them. His new lifestyle was probably bankrolled by these affairs. What Sebastian couldn't figure out was why Xavi would tell him they were after his house. He didn't protect any of the men in his waiting room. Xavi's whole endeavor could be at risk by telling Sebastian.

He felt the need to let it all go. Erasure simplified things. It allowed him the space to create something new. Even though he had nothing with which to replace what would be lost, he wanted it gone. The feeling resembled the one that welled within him years ago when he left his father. Now, Xavi and his legacy were the subject. He wondered how easy it would be to reinvent himself again.

Sebastian and Xavi arrived at the port, not the old port with its shifting freight labyrinth, but the new one being constructed at its edges, creeping along the shoreline of the city. A string of waterfront restaurants and bars lined the expanse before him. Each had a section of tables cordoned off from the neighboring establishments and pedestrians. Waiters in black ties and neatly ironed shirts darted in and out carrying drinks and seafood. The din of conversation from couples and other parties filled the air, redolent with the scent of the sea. Lines of boats moored at the edge of the port. Docks in all shapes reached out before a large building floating further out. In the distance, a bridge connected the floating shopping mall a hundred meters out.

An array of white tables was spread across the even, grey, cobbled expanse that led to the moored boats. The cafes that owned them were lined up next to each other snugly and formed a rectangular ring about the port. Sebastian could not tell the difference between one café and the next, so identical and snug they were. These cafes were alive with the buzz of humanity in the summer, but as the seasons were wearing on in a slow exhaustive breath, it was rather desolate this day. The slight chill from the sea was enough to drive people from its path. Most found comfort in their strolls between parallel shops, warmed by the warmth of others.

The gulls squawked away floating buoyantly in the sunlight. Their wings arched, their white bodies drifted with the currents of sea breeze moving invisibly in the air. The sea's motion could be heard. Sebastian could almost feel its waves lapping upon the bulwarks. He watched the gulls for a moment more, then returned.

Sebastian walked down into the din of the cafes toward the boats following Xavi. Someone called out to Xavi. He didn't stop, moving forward briskly and not looking at the scene around him. Sebastian scanned the crowd and found an arm extended up, waving in their direction. He caught Xavi by the elbow and pointed toward the owner. Xavi broke free and scowled at Sebastian for stalling him. Arturo, Grey's aide, and two large men wearing suits approached from the table. Xavi noticed them and seemed on the verge of running but the crowd was too thick for him to leave.

"Hello Xavi. Grey has been waiting for you. Please proceed," Arturo said.

"Grey has been expecting you," one of the suits said.

"Please come with us," the other added.

Sebastian began to follow Xavi but was stopped by a gesture from Arturo. "Mr. Veillard, a moment of your time." Xavi continued forward leaving Sebastian and Arturo alone.

Arturo spoke in clearly enunciated, crisp words that never ran together. His mannerisms matched his attire — freshly pressed, without a wrinkle in his suit. Arturo's neck and limbs were thin. Sebastian could break past the toothpick if it came down to it.

"Time. It's curious. People have marked it differently over the centuries. The ancient Romans thought it ordinal. It started at one end and finished at another. I think we view it differently now. It's fluid. Our perceptions of it change based on our internal clocks. The vantage from which we see an object determines its relation to us. Mr. Grey doesn't know how to manipulate circumstances, so I do all the collection of time."

"You stopped me for this?"

"I thought you would understand. You've seen the lost generation, one trapped by time. They don't even realize how dangerous they are, how loose they are from the history of previous realities."

"What are you talking about?"

"I thought the doctor's office would have clued you in. Then there's Opal."

Sebastian squared off with the aide. "What do you know about Julía?"

"This rebellion, the loss of houses, all of it is planned. Opal knew that. They're loosening up bits of time ready to be collected."

"Collected how?"

"Collected by persons like me. Persons like you too, if you care to. I know you'll see the way soon enough. Just think of what you can gain. People are just giving time away, not just their own but time from the past too. I want you to infiltrate the protestors. They fancy themselves part of a revolt of sorts. Listen to their words. Among them, they are said to have found an aleph. I want to know about any that exist. Tell me where it is if you can."

"What do I receive in return?"

Arturo adjusted his cufflinks. "You'll find your father. If you find an aleph, he'll be close by. Think of me now and again, will you? I'd like to think you're on our side, the side collecting time. Remember alephs. They exist. You'd do well to find one."

Others had seen one. Arturo was right, just like his father. Finding one meant his father was still out in the city somewhere, but now he was in front of Grey. "Now is not the time."

Sebastian walked past the strange little man to where Xavi sat with Grey.

Xavi nodded to Sebastian and resumed conversation with the members of the party, having lost interest in Sebastian for the moment. Trays of fresh oysters lined the table full with cocktails, some in champagne glasses, others in highballs. The slices of lemon on the trays stood out as yellow flecks on an otherwise white tabletop. Sebastian recognized one of the men from the construction site at the table. His attention focused on two women surrounding who acted fascinated at his every word. A miniature dog sat in the purse resting on one of their laps. The others seemed engaged in their own affairs quite apart from the one Grey began from the far side of the table.

"Xavi, I was hoping to see you. Please join us. Sebastian, you too."

They withdrew two of the silver metal chairs and sat. The escorts remained standing behind the two men.

"I heard you were leaving, Xavi. I thought to myself, I can't let him leave without showing him off. We have to celebrate. Drinks." He called over to the waiters and ordered two more drinks for them. "So I set up our little party here where we would find you. Quite smart of me don't you think?"

The foreman agreed and his two companions laughed. Xavi sat uneasily. All his loquaciousness had dissipated. He shifted anxiously in his chair and avoided eye contact with the members of the table.

"And you Sebastian, where have you been? My foreman says you disappeared from the work I sent you. It reflects badly on me to recommend someone who has such a poor work ethic."

"That's not what happened. What are you doing out there?"

"Sebastian, not now," Xavi interjected.

"Doing? We're helping this city grow. What else would we be doing?"

The dog began growling at Xavi.

"The people who are going missing, you're behind it."

"Sebastian."

Grey laughed. It was a low sort of chuckle, one that seemed racked with bile and the layers of fat on his body. "I'm behind people who are going missing. And your father, I suppose I made him disappear as well." No one at the table seemed to notice. If anything, they were amused by his speech. "I don't have that kind of power, Sebastian. Such accusations are absurd. People missing in the city. They probably moved on to a better life. Isn't that right, Xavi? There are so many opportunities. No one wants to stay in their tenement apartments when they find a better paying job. Maybe they're leaving their old lives behind. Don't want to be reminded of the past they had. Not one bit."

"I don't believe you."

"I'm not going to entertain your ridiculous fantasies."

Sebastian thought back to the images he had seen underground. They had no bearing up here. He still couldn't understand how the girl knew what was going on. It led him straight to Xavi, and now Grey. There was no way he could explain how he knew. His recourse was limited.

"Listen, before you go, I've heard about your little trip. There are some things I need you to wrap up. I can't have everything running smoothly with you away. You owe me that much, Xavi. Sebastian, can you imagine how much of a mess things would be if Xavi left? The whole city would fall apart. We can't have that now, can we?"

Xavi adjusted his seat in the chair, his eyes averted from the others, his neck twitching slightly.

"Sebastian, go on. I'll detain Xavi here for a bit as we settle things."

One of the escorts placed a hand on Sebastian's shoulder. He stood and took a few steps away under their guidance. He stopped and looked back at Xavi. His jaw was clenched shut. Sebastian could see the outline of his bone structure strained under his skin. His eyes were still averted. A girl laughed at the conversation running on the opposite side of the table. She did not notice Sebastian.

"Oh, Sebastian, there's one last thing. I'll give you another chance to set things right. There's another project that could use your help. Arturo." Grey wrote something on a small pad of paper and tore it from the book. Arturo bore it to Sebastian. "It's the site I want you to see. Be sure to go tomorrow."

Xavi's boat was somewhere in the distance. It was where he wanted to go before Grey intercepted them. Sebastian decided to look for it.

He thought about Julía and how she claimed to have lost all sense of herself. Did that happen to his father too? To everyone in this city who disappeared? He wished he had an idea of how to find her.

His feet plodded one after another through the realization that Julía and his father shared the same fate. He went toward the light reflected on the water, drawn by the flow of the sea. The din created by the diners diminished and Sebastian stepped onto the platform by the water. By the edge near the wooden deck, the bridge connected the floating mall. A few benches lined the side on a lower level. Young couples sat huddled together on benches by the water. A few boys entertained themselves by dropping rocks into the sea and watching them sink. Their attention wandered in boredom to whoever passed by. The bravest of them would call out, mocking anyone who looked meek in his eyes.

The sea's turbulent motion never ceased as it was pulled from the ends of the world. Sebastian wondered if the same drops were forever in this port, or if they, too, meandered, continually changing, continually moving.

His upturned head slowly fell to the streets around him. It looked a new place, one he had never seen before. He strode forward with curiosity exploring the world as it unfolded before him. He departed the port leaving Xavi sitting uncomfortably with Grey. He was oblivious to the men who followed in tow after him.

The sea was replete with beauty and life as so many of the people here lived by its motion. Its ululating rhythm beat through the ground, hushing the minds of all who felt it as its rush and hiss played in the air. This pace could soothe the people here. It had the ability to guide them as the moon went and came, again and again in an endless cycle.

But there was something more that had been forgotten. It was a collective amnesia upon which their lives had been built. This modern world had trembled like a mirage in all its foreign brilliance. The shiny baubles in glittering window panes and allure of glaring nightlights betrayed the antiquated splendor. Once the image dissipated, a harder, grittier existence spoke otherwise.

The shore was populated by intermittent palms that looked desolate in a sea of concrete. A broad avenue ran the shore's length, before the walk that overlooked to the quay. The sea breeze tousled the palm fronds idly in the afternoon air. Sebastian listened to the fronds thrash without complaint. The sun had burned away the morning's dew. The sky was now clear with a peace that hid the tidings of things to come. The sea could be heard everywhere around him. He looked at the boats tethered at a nearby port. A cobbled walkway led up to the docks and ended abruptly.

In this contemptible state, Sebastian stared dumbly at his surroundings. His head hung about him like a beaten dog. He wandered the plaza several times and found no solace from his plight. The place was full of an air of Dionysian delight. The garishly hued canvas of life dizzied him with smells and sights he never recalled seeing. He looked at its surface, all agog at the things he had never experienced or dreamed before.

There were soldierly lines of bottles in their myriad intoxicating colors displayed at every café where people dined and laughed under the night's air. Such order was out of place in this reeling world. He no longer understood it, or perhaps, it was himself that he no longer knew. Sebastian was confronted by his image contorted on the bottles' bulbous bodies. It looked back at him sadly as yet another passing image in this too fleeting world. His eyes were weary. He cringed at the dwindling image of himself he saw. He reached out. His own mammoth hand replaced the image in a futile attempt to touch something real and tangible. A bartender interrupted him and he went back to wandering. The myriad faces of the crowd multiplied his solitude. He recoiled, feeling lost and afraid in an abyss of sensation.

He ran along the pier, now in sight of the sea. Straight along the planks he went, passing boat and passenger along the way, until he reached the end of the pier where without hesitation, without breaking step in his pace, he dove into the sea.

Its luminescent body sparkled with millions of tiny suns. They came into existence and died all in an instant of the eye. Its brilliance was so glorious that he felt blinded by it. He closed his eyes and breathed. Bobbing among the waves, the scent of the air invigorated his lungs. He could taste the spray in the back of his throat. Slowly at first, he moved his arms, propelling him ever forward on the roving mass of water. It tossed about with a life all its own, and he among it, making his way as part of the myriad other particles tossing about in the brilliant tumult of the sea. His arms picked up speed. He forgot himself. Lost in the motion of the sea, he moved without thought or concern for who or where he was. All that existed was himself and the sea. The world became quiet save for the sounds of his breaths emerging into a world of sunlight, then disappearing in the world of water beneath. Sebastian moved in this manner for what seemed an eternity.

As dusk fell on the port, he dove down into the water, below the glow of neon on the water. He swam down away from the waves above. Below, statues of men and women stood on the sea floor. Fish darted in and out of the stone structures. Sebastian paused to look at some seaweed stretched around one figure like a scarf. His breath became tight and he propelled himself upward to the surface — another world from the cast statues below.

Were they real people? Did Grey cast the dispossessed in stone? Or were they something older, something forgotten? Sebastian would never know. He had enough trouble focusing on the here and now. Mysteries of the past were too elusive to the lightning rod the city had become.

When he finally tired, his head arose from the water, and spotting some land nearby, he swam towards it without a thought in his mind.

III

Rebellion was in the air. Even the rats could smell it. You saw them scurrying along the uneven streets of the Old Quarter. They hopped the tapestry of stonework as if thunder clapped underfoot, announcing a flood of water to come. The water would run and thrash through the network of stones in a downpour that led straight to the gutter. The heat ready to break, a downpour waited, puffed up just above the red roofs of the city, lingering in the space between the sea and the dry buildings leading up to the shore. Sebastian knew it was coming well before the first drops began to splatter from on high. They hit, one then another, onto the stonework, the tiles of roofs, on bald statues, on people's feet as they crossed the promenade, even on umbrellas.

Sebastian stood, hair on end with electricity in the air threatening to strike.

Every one of Sebastian's senses knew it was coming. The past few weeks told him to expect turmoil. Now it took form from the coolness of the city brushing up against the dry heat of the land. The city stood on a precipice — which way it fell was yet to be determined. The events to come would be revolutionary and Sebastian knew where he stood in relation to them.

Pavel gathered up a stack of flattened cardboard boxes. He sat them next to Sebastian as he plastered posters along a wall. The sheets formed a solid rectangle: a man's height and twenty meters long. They read "Make Art, Not War," in red and black lettering. Each faced out to the sidewalk where pedestrians would pass, reading propaganda for one agenda or another. Sebastian knew with certainty on which side he stood.

"Let's go," Pavel said.

The rain came down. It fell heavily onto the cardboard Pavel tucked under his arm. The two walked through the warren of streets in the Old Quarter toward the nearest metro at Museo.

"We're going to find her, you know."

Sebastian did not respond. He didn't pick up his head from the stairs he walked down. Grime covered ceramic tile at the edges. His feet squeaked as the ceiling of the metro station covered his head. Opal had been gone for weeks now. There was no clue to his father either. His only course was to join Pavel, Rodrigo, and the others in their struggle to aid their missing family and friends. He couldn't stomach working for Grey after the meeting at the port. He knew too much about how Grey transformed the landscape to be a part of the reconstruction of the city.

Some thought they should fight the system. Others, like Pavel, were content to keep searching. But they all felt something — anger, loss, emptiness, a need for change. Something had to give in the city. They all knew it was coming and braced to act on the momentum, wherever it may take them.

Sebastian tried to be fluid, to be flexible, like wind. He tried to be pliant as he moved along the platform. "No one finds anything in this city anymore. It's a lost cause for a lost generation. We can only remember the ones that got away."

Pavel grimaced as they stood on the platform, waiting for a lighted train to pass. "We'll make it. We have to."

Sebastian shook his head. "No one sees anything in this city anymore."

They lowered themselves down onto the tracks and walked along the rails.

"It's as if this whole city has gone blind to this epidemic."

Sebastian never should have trusted Xavi. Sebastian knew he was too trusting now. He wouldn't make the same mistakes.

They traversed the tunnel to the old train car where Pavel lived. Sebastian sat in the back while Pavel piled the cardboard near the entrance. He had a number of materials he would bring down from above to use in his search for his sister.

Sebastian curled up on the metro seat and pulled out his father's journal to read.

It was beginning to make sense. Sebastian could see through the rambling of the old man and make connections between the phenomena they both witnessed. Sebastian licked his finger to turn the page. His eyes devoured the next text.

He withdrew his own journal to write about his discoveries.

I'm documenting this so that I don't lose any more information. Like my father ... he went mad. He confronted the same forces I am facing now. It broke him. Every day I am more convinced that he shared the same fate as those I saw underground. It's hard to face, but I can't come up with any other conclusion.

Through his writings, I came to understand the circumstances in which I now find myself. Without him, none of this would have been possible to conceive of. I would have found out nothing. He was the first to stand up as far as I can tell. The burden was too much and he crumbled. I must be cautious to prevent the same from happening to me.

Already I have noticed myself losing time. I am in one place then moments later I find myself in entirely new environs. I have no memory of how I moved from one place to the other. When I look at the calendar on my phone, days have passed. The messages on it tell me who I've been in contact with, but none of the names are recognizable. For instance I know that I met with a Pietro two days ago but I have no idea what we talked about. The messages insinuate that something is being planned, but I have no idea as to what.

These instances happen more and more often. The week becomes a moth-eaten scarf, unfurled and toothless with days missing out of it. I write this in the hopes of piecing things together, of maintaining some sanity as I come to understand what is happening in this city.

Opal — the search begins with her. She seems complicit with Grey somehow. I've almost given up on my father. Since the day at the port, Xavi has gone missing. Opal does not even know who Xavi is anymore. How is this possible? I need to find Xavi as well. Opal will lead me to him and then to my father.

He hadn't spent much time at his house the last few weeks. It was in as much disrepair as Pavel's underground hideaway. At least, Pavel's home had electricity and company. Every so often he would emerge back onto the streets above to look at his old house. He couldn't go in. The memories were too strong for him. He did not want to think about his mother any more. Her death had plagued him for too long and if he stayed in the house it would be like resting in a corpse, especially as he found out what his father did to her.

It was too painful for Sebastian to stay in the house any more. Too many ghosts lived in the woodwork waiting to be discovered. The answers Sebastian sought couldn't be found there. They existed outside in the city somewhere. He had to keep searching. Finding Julía was the only action that would give him some peace. He had given up on his father. At least Julía still existed.

Since his return, Sebastian had developed a new attachment to the city. The mysteries in the city bore too much intrigue. There was no way he could return to South America now, not until he had some closure with affairs.

Sebastian would sit in the Placa after viewing his house.

He began looking at waiters differently. As they brought him coffee and croissants, he questioned if they were actually waiters, if they actually were spying on him, ferreting information to someone else who knew more than he did. He sipped the coffee questionably, half believing it could be drugged with some kind of narcotic. The croissants he would tear into pieces, feeding pigeons clandestinely before eating.

When Sebastian walked down the street, he was not sure of the difference between tourists and street performers. The street performers wore garish costumes and posed for money, but they could just as easily have been visiting the world of the everyday from their respective enclaves of their characters' lives. At what point did the life of an entertainer eclipse that of the person behind the mask? Sebastian did not know anymore.

The tourists taking pictures and buying souvenirs were equally as disconcerting, for they had a presence that never seemed to abate. For people who were supposedly from another place, they never seemed to leave. Sebastian suspected that they were actually residents of the city who posed as tourists, but for what purpose? Could they be enthusiastically enthralled with the same wonders of the city, or, did they merely pose as tourists to affect a sense of novelty in their daily interactions. Perhaps it was worse. They could suffer from the amnesia that seemed to be plaguing this town. They could be ordinary people who have lost all recollection of who they are, and hence are perpetually entertained by the places they will see every day for the remainder of their lives.

Sebastian began to think that the tradition from which he came had never existed. It was a heat vapor that makes the air shimmer, creating a mirage of tourists follow.

These thoughts and others agitated Sebastian. He was becoming unhinged. In his derangement, he lost sight of anything that he may have been obligated to do. He spent his time continually wandering the streets, searching for some shred of truth in the city he had once held as his home.

All he saw were traces. Traces of footprints in the gravel of parks. Traces of people walking, their presence like wind — an absence in the air. Traces of clothing discarded like crumbs in the street. Everywhere Sebastian went the missing filled space with absence. He felt them missing in rooms. He saw them in wistful glances at empty stools. He saw them in the elderly walking along with hands paired behind backs. In dogs leashed to trees on the Promenade. There were traces everywhere, traces of absence in the sand of time.

2

Sebastian met Xavi's assistant near the border of the Old Quarter and the Promenade. At the entrance to the square, a car had pulled off onto the upper end of the V formed by the cobbled streets so runoff could drain from the square. It blocked most of the way forward in the shade of the surrounding buildings save for a half meter. Luggage and other belongings were tied to the roof of the compact. He leaned in to her open window. "Here. This is what he wanted right? Will it help him leave?"

"I don't know. He's still missing. I had to get it for him, before I took off. It's the last thing I can do to help ease things for him. You know how it goes."

"So you're leaving too? I can't say I blame you."

She stepped out of the car, making a show of tightening the ropes on the roof of her car. Inside Sebastian saw recording devices and computer screens, long microphones and receivers among bundled sleeping bags and boxes of cereal.

"What's with the equipment?"

"You do things you're not proud of to survive, but at least you survive. He asked me to watch. Underneath it all, he did care for you, as much as anyone could. Besides, this is the least of the things I had to do. I'm leaving. I've had enough of this place. I don't care if people know about what's been going on. Maybe I can get some cash for the devices. I need to get out."

She tightened the rigging on top of the car. "There's nothing here for me anymore. Xavi's disappeared. I can be someone else, someplace else. Hopefully I can find some peace away from this place. It's racked me for too long. It's racked everyone. The things people have done. The things they get away with. I can't face it. It's too sad."

"They can't silence everyone. Even if this city is changing, leaving only makes the problem worse. You're walking away. You had a hand in this. Xavi was in it up to his eyes and you knew. Leaving now makes you more of a coward."

"That's funny coming from you. You left. You abandoned this place first. You even sold your house. Besides, I'd rather be a living coward than a dead hero."

Two police approached the car from the opposite end of the street. "Looks like it's time." She put it in gear and drove toward the Promenade. Sebastian stepped back as the police began approaching her car.

The police had been accosting everybody lately. Sebastian couldn't call it martial law, but the state police made a stronger show in the Old Quarter these days. Too many anarchists and protestors interfered with the tourist traffic. Stefanie, with her car full of electronic equipment, begged to be stopped. They tried to catch her before she entered the main street. Sometimes they let you go, other times they took everything you had. Bribery was common among the city officials.

You sold your house. These words echoed in his head as she got into her car and started the ignition. Again, he had lost time. The engine roared and the car began rumbling over the cobbled street. In the interim he had sold his house according to Xavi's assistant. At the intersection, a car stopped short just past the entryway, allowing only the front of Stefanie's car out. From behind, a bus careened into the driver's door. The three vehicles bent like an accordion into wreckage.

Stefanie's car buckled between the two. Drivers emerged from nearby cars to look at the accident. The sounds of horns filled the air, one permanently depressed. Visions of his mother came back to him. She had died similarly in traffic at the border of the Old Quarter and the Expansion. Sebastian watched as traffic sped past on the other side of the palm-lined boulevard. His head felt heavy. He tilted his head up, hoping to see what had happened. His steps quickened into a jog. As he got to the assistant's car, he saw blood spattered on the cracked windshield. Cracks ran down the glass in a spiderweb pattern. He tried to pull his head together but too much happened at the same time. The driver's side had crumpled by the impact of the bus. The other collided with a lamppost on the sidewalk and bent in two. Xavi's assistant sat dead in the driver's seat. Her head lay on the wheel, split open, blood pouring onto the floor and seat.

His mother. His mother died like this. She stepped out of the confines of the Old Quarter to be run down by the traffic of the Promenade. He looked to the bus driver. The man gestured frantically at the mess from his seat. Passengers exited the bus and complained to him. Some rubbed their necks and spines. In front, the car that stopped short had escaped most of the impact. The lamppost absorbed most of the velocity from behind. Only a small dent in the bumper showed any impact. Next to the first car, before all the chaos clogging the street, the horns blaring, the bus passengers complaining, and traffic piling up behind, Mizu stood. Pavel went up to her and embraced her before the crowd. The family reunion seemed bittersweet — lost family members ebbing forth from the crowd. Pavel thanked god and kissed his sister. She had been lost for weeks now.

She stood aloof, almost as if in shock at the accident. Her eyes ran over the crumpled metal behind her uncomprehendingly. She traced a bird in flight as it landed on one of the trees in the median, chirping over the confusion in the street below.

Horns blared. Spectators gathered. Sirens rang in the distance, blocked by pedestrian and street traffic.

"She was just trying to leave. Where have you been? Why didn't you stop?"

"What are you talking about?"

Sebastian looked past the crumpled front end into Mizu's car. The registration fell out of the glove compartment. The vehicle was registered to the Grey

Corporation. Sebastian covered his face with his hands. "I can't. I can't. Not now. Not you too."

"Why is there all this traffic?"

He muttered to himself. "Why? Why Xavi? You shouldn't have let this happen." He bit his fist and hit a nearby car. His hand left a small dent in the metal that glinted with light from the sun. Onlookers from the crowd gathering began to look at him.

Sebastian felt himself becoming unhinged. "Don't you know what he's doing to this city? He's erasing it, from the ground up. It's unrecognizable. Don't you care about anything that's been lost?"

She stared at him as if nothing had happened, as if they shared no past, no history.

The bus driver walked up behind them and started shouting.

"It's not safe here."

The gathering crowd created a tense environment that would only get worse. Sebastian pictured emergency officials prying the assistant's dead body from the wreck. People would gawk at the spectacle, some even take pictures. Why are they drawn to such tragedy? he thought. It's as if looking in the face of death relieved their own doubts at what would happen at the end of the human dance. There were no answers. He saw none. Too much suffering occurred in the steps for him to worry about when the music stopped. He had to live in this moment, only this one. If he made it through the moment he lived in, he could go on to the next and the one after without having to weigh the infinite past and future surrounding him.

You sold your house. How could it have happened? Sebastian had no idea. These times, these missing periods of memory dotted the last few weeks. He hoped he hadn't. He needed the house. Right now, more than anything he needed to see it — his mother's house.

Sebastian thought of his mother; of how she died in traffic; of how life can end so suddenly. Part of him crumpled with the car — the part that knew Xavi would have mourned her death. An image of his mother came to him. His head twitched at the thought. Death was so close. It seemed to be everywhere around him. He did not think he could handle seeing Opal's corpse. Not in the same way as Xavi's assistant. There was too much loss in this world.

He stared open-faced at the traffic jam building around the accident. He needed to leave, to find some calmer spot that would not leave him unhinged. He thought back to his house. It was all he had left of his mother.

His mother died similarly in the mix of traffic in the Promenade. How much longer would people stream through it? It was only a matter of time before the street would be redrawn by the growth of the city. He wanted to leave — to be somewhere familiar once again.

Pavel, Mizu and Sebastian left the site of the wreckage. The noise followed them as it reverberated horns, murmurings and sirens behind them in the streets of the Old Quarter.

3

The houses being demolished for luxury lofts were now luxury lofts being demolished for raw materials. The crew was not involved in the process of constructing but of deconstructing the landscape into its most basic materials. Copper spools were hauled off to trucks. Blocks of cement walls were piled in organized sections to be sorted through later. Near the top of the structure, a crane pulled the steel girders one by one from the excavated innards of the building. If what he had seen earlier in his stay was the need for growth, the scene he witnessed now was a cannibalization of that earlier dream.

He saw the foreman he talked to earlier organizing how to dismantle the building of which, days ago, he had orchestrated the construction. Crews moved in organized groups according to the materials they gathered. Copper crews stripped the wires from the walls. Cement men swung hammers at piles of concrete that were knocked from the building by cranes. The steel crew worked in the distance, far atop the structure, guiding the crane to rip girders from the top and place them on trucks that ferreted the material away.

The foreman did not look concerned that his efforts were being dismantled. In fact, he seemed quite pleased with himself. He sat counting money as wall after wall fell down from the building he worked to erect the week before.

It was a continual process in which the city dwelt — one of construction and deconstruction.

*

A sudden movement caught his eye as he crossed the entranceway of a nearby completed building's lobby. He turned and found himself looking at a ghostly figure. A face drawn thin, a patched network of wrinkles on his brow, and mercurial eyes that searched endlessly composed the face before him. It had a resemblance to his father. That searching look was the one he imagined late at night in the study as he pored over the journals. How had the man been reduced to such a gaunt figure? Sebastian thought. He neared closer and reached out almost to touch the man who peered intently back at him. The man, too, reached, and the tips of their fingers caressed the glass of the mirror. Sebastian drew back. He was becoming the lost ones he imagined.

"Sir, the door is over there."

The receptionist stirred him from this haunting vision. Sebastian stepped away from the mirror and muttered a thank you.

"It's always a pleasure to see you, sir." The receptionist smiled warmly at him from behind her desk. He pushed the entrance doors out of his way and into the streets. It was only after he had walked blocks away, when he was outside the metro stairs searching for a cigarette in his pockets, that he realized it was the first time he had been there.

He needed clarity in the tangle of strings leading him along. Xavi tried to warn him, but he also was a collaborator. The construction made no sense. Buildings went up. Workers cannibalized them. The process started all over again. Why would anyone do that? Someone had to know about the scams going on, all over the city it seemed. Sebastian speculated that some of the officials must be bribed to turn a blind eye to the contracts that were never fulfilled, or fulfilled late.

The receptionist's words stuck with him. How had she known him? What games were they playing? They meant to unnerve him, to shake his concentration so that they could hide something, but exactly what that was he was not sure.

Sebastian sat at the base of a tall stature erected at the base of the Promenade. He leaned his back against the cool marble and stared out to sea. A few odd couples sat kissing or huddled on benches. The light from streetlamps and late night clubs shone on the dappling water. He brushed his hand against the ground and felt grainy deposits from the pedestrian traffic that coursed through the streets during the day. His hand raised, Sebastian inspected the tiny black particles. They stuck to the base of his palm, near where the creases in his hand ended. He rubbed the grime between his fingers, eager to feel something tangible. So much was out of reach in this city.

He walked along the boardwalk and peered over the railing. He spotted one of the vagrant occupants of the city. A pair of spindly legs protruded from under the walk. Sebastian descended the nearest staircase to investigate. A cement walk had been constructed below the boardwalk above. It was littered with trash and waste. Sebastian saw some old men sitting on upturned plastic paint buckets playing dominoes on a similarly upturned cardboard box.

The man Sebastian sought was sprawled in a mess on the ground. He was nestled atop a collection of oddities that appeared to be his. Various sized TV's, glass jars, and used batteries were his cushions among other disposed things.

They lived free from the constraints of an established society. Sebastian couldn't help but wonder if they were truly free. These people lived collectively. They shared all they had, consuming it with the pleasure of indulgence. Large groups of them would occupy abandoned buildings claiming them as their own. They tried to live apart from the moored aspects of society, not acknowledging their subsistence from its wealth. They lived through begging money from tourists and the bourgeois and selling drugs. He would see them migrate in the nights from places like this corner in twos and threes to squares like the Placa. Late at night they would cavort there for long hours. Their bodies lined the steps in numbers, blocking the plaque of a statue of a man in its center. It was covered in graffiti. Sebastian wondered if the symbols made it their home or defamed that which they did not understand. He thought it was ironic to deface a man who believed in their ideals. Perhaps it was praise. The next day rubbish and broken glass littered the square. Sebastian remembered the shopkeepers who swept the remaining debris every morning shaking their head with the grimace of work. Was this the way to live freely?

A man on a bike pulled up next to Sebastian. He unslung a messenger bag from his shoulder and withdrew a long cylindrical case. The man extended the slender, cylindrical messenger tube toward Sebastian. His arm outstretched imploringly as if its extension depended on Sebastian's acceptance. Sebastian knew he had never seen the man before.

"Here's the documents you asked for, Mr. Veillard."

'What?"

"The documents. You told me to deliver them to you here last week."

"I've never seen you before."

"You asked me to meet you here. One week ago, sir."

"I've never met you before."

"Just take them. You said you'd say that. You told me to tell you this is what you're looking for. Look, if you don't take 'em, I don't get paid. Sign this." The man pushed a sheet of paper in Sebastian's face. He scribbled his name. The messenger detached a flimsy carbon copy and left before the rioters took over the streets.

Sebastian took the tube and unrolled the plans within. He surveyed the plans. Inside, the layout for a massive commercial complex encompassing the The Old Quarter was drawn in white lines over the blue paper. His house stood in the middle of the proposed plan. Sebastian looked to interrogate the messenger more but the man had already mounted his bike and pedaled off along the coast. The sun scintillated off the silver parts of his bike, blinding Sebastian occasionally with the light reflected from the moving parts of metal. His eyes drew back toward the sea.

How had he known? If it was the only occurrence, Sebastian would not have given it any thought, but, these oddities happened more frequently every day. First the city changed over a month, then people began disappearing, now he couldn't remember things he had done. No. There must be someone else. A double, doppelganger, someone posed as him to get these plans; but why? He had met Julía's double, and seen something resembling his father too. It was not much of a stretch to imagine there was a copy of him out there, masquerading in his life.

His house stood at the center of much of the land already under contract.

*

He had the dogged feeling of pursuit hovering over him as the three walked through the Old Quarter. Sebastian stifled the urge to look over his shoulder, or peer around corners. The effort would not do him any good. No matter which way he turned, someone would be watching. He was sure of that now. The confines of the city seemed to contract around him. The walls of the buildings seemed to creep forward, inching toward him while his head was turned. The stones underfoot moved too. One by one the cobbled stones would raise a few centimeters. He stumbled more than once on these raised obstructions. His toes began to feel numb from how often he stubbed them. Mizu helped him up each time. She held his arm and helped raise him from the street.

He had the feeling that the streets moved. When he turned to check for landmarks, the entrance to a side street moved back. The distance had elongated since he last looked. The Old Quarter became a place of contortions to him. The landscape of the place changed too much. He felt confined by it, imprisoned by the old gothic spires, the tall wooden doors, the iron latticework above, the stones underneath — it all held him, shackled him to a past that no longer was. Sebastian yearned to be free from his confinement. Still, eyes watched him. He was sure of it.

From that point on Sebastian's frame bent. Sebastian had to know whether his desire to erase his past had finally happened. They ran through the streets, losing themselves in the warren of the Old Quarter on their way to his house. They became lost and Sebastian stepped into a café hidden deep inside its edges to ask for directions. Sebastian went to the restroom while Mizu sat at a table. He ran the faucet. The water was cold. It shook in his hands before he splashed his face. Beads dripped down his cheek. He looked at himself in the mirror. A strange face stared back at him. He walked out to Pavel who had ordered three shots of espresso. He handed Sebastian one and asked if he was all right.

"Fine," he said. Mizu left to go to the ladies' room and he drank his coffee. He could not believe her nonchalance. It was as if she had no recognition beyond the moment she was in. Everything that happened before or after had no consequence. She lived in a bubble of the moment, never thinking beyond the present state. Everyone around him was either dying or disappearing, being replaced by vacant doubles, frail husks of their former selves.

A man sitting at a table with wicker-backed chairs spoke to him. He cracked pistachios as he talked. The shells scattered all across the table; the man fed the nuts to a parakeet hopping amid the debris. It chirped with each half.

"Every generation is succeeded by something new. We can't hold onto what we know. We remember the city a certain way. This is a dream. You and I believe the place in which we live to be concrete, to be fixed. We feel the stones under our feet, the smell of salt in the air, and feel the sun burning wrinkles into our skin. But this world is not the one in which we live. It is a construct of our minds, one that not everyone sees. No, our city is being replaced. It has been replaced ten times over since you and I began talking. It is still being replaced constantly. With every new burgeoning rush to seize the palpable moments that remind us we are alive, someone new makes this city his own. That's why you don't recognize me and I don't recognize you. That's why you get lost in a city you should know. It's changing, beyond your control, into something new. What can we do? You can sit there and cry about it, or you can finish your coffee, walk out into the street, inhale the breeze, watch women walk down the street, admire the new clothes in shop windows and make this place your own."

The man placed the meat of a pistachio in front of the parakeet. Its beak opened and ate the nut. A pleased chirp arose from it. Sebastian did not understand what the man said. His brows furrowed. He stared at the man, uncertain whether he felt frightened or excited by these new possibilities. His head turned quickly. Sebastian stared at the stark light breaking into the shade of the café. People ambled past in the street. They moved with a grace that ignored the doubt that ran through Sebastian's head, paralyzing him in a state between action and inaction. He teetered between these two states, unable to make a decision. At once his body seemed wound tight enough to run from the café and emerge into the street at an inestimable pace, one that could not be stopped no matter what effort was exerted against it. At the same instant, he felt chained. His legs could not move even if he tried to exert himself. So great was his apprehension that his synapses ceased responding. His toes perched on the balls of his skeleton. The pressure built. He felt as if he might topple, so great was the tension between acting and not acting. His body had relented on a cellular level.

"Remember," the man said.

The hum of construction greeted them as they found the square where Sebastian's house stood since his absence. Men and machines covered the square. A crane's arm reached toward his house. People darted in and out. Workers hauled lumber out from the house — floorboards, copper wire, glass — anything that could be salvaged. Sebastian watched as they slowly gutted the house, the structure becoming skeletal over the course of a few hours. Some walked on the roof prying loose clay red tiles. The supplies created a neatly stacked array according to type. He sat, trying to comprehend the action. All throughout the day, he had been compelled to watch. He could not turn no matter how many times Mizu tried to urge him away. He could not understand why the deconstruction could hold sway over him so completely. He tried accessing memories that informed him of the place, but the scene before him was so jarring that he could not go past the surface of events. Trucks rumbled along the street, one after another. being loaded until their beds were full. One would drive off and another took its place. At the end of the day, nothing remained of the house. The skeletal frame dismantled, empty space occupied the place where Sebastian was raised. When the workers finished, the collapse of the house produced a small sound like an exhalation. Joints cracked until they gave way like old tendons. When the frame fell, bulldozers moved in and began carting the debris away. A few workmen directed traffic around the site. Pathways began to emerge into the site. The men walked in, pointing out new piles to be removed and sorted.

"But this is my house."

Sebastian left his seat at the curb across the square and meandered through the streets. Mizu followed him through the din of cafés and shoppers. Tourists flashed pictures. He was becoming stranger by the day. Fits like this one seized him more often.

The avenues drove on into occasional plazas where they split diagonally, or squarely around some statue, fountain, or treed expanse where some old man watched it all from his seat on a bench, or along a gravel path through which he walked with his lone grandchild, the gravel crumpling under his traveled feet.

He stumbled out a pathetic "It's all lost," and the life of a breath wheezed out of his slumping form.

"But you lived them once. They'll always be with you. In some remote form or another, those experiences are part of you now. They are who you are. And those places? They still exist. They're out there, somewhere in the world. The air we're breathing here is touched by them in some way. You can always visit them again."

He lost his way in the Old Quarter. It changed too quickly for him to map out the network of changing streets and buildings. It took him twice as long to find places he should have known. Sometimes they didn't exist any more, like the school.

4

He came to face a park at the border of the Old Quarter. The Parc Ciudad connected to the far end of the Old Quarter where its streets fed into the industrial cargo sector running parallel to the sea. It hosted a zoo with an albino gorilla. When Sebastian was a boy the ape had come to stay in the city. The ape was cast out in the wild for being so distinct. He found a life as a show to zoo visitors. Sebastian wanted to relive the days when he first met the ape. He traveled to see him in the park. The gravel crushed under his feet. Two rows of metal cages contained dusty felines. Sebastian wondered at a life of spectacle. He did not think it would be for him. Each of these animals was on display when they napped or ate, never a moment to themselves save when they slept or the zoo closed.

He found the gorilla, an old white majestic animal, slowly chewing a stick. He ground it into splinters in his teeth. Sebastian thought the gorilla at the end of his life. The animal bore more creases in his face than Sebastian remembered. To spend twenty years in a cage, he could not imagine. He felt sorrow for the animal — so human in appearance, yet so powerful. This albino ape — cast out from his social group — survived only in captivity. Sebastian thought to his father who had taken him here as a child. He held Sebastian's hand as they strolled between cages toward the gorilla's home. Then Sebastian did not have the same curiosity for the animal. He though of the newness of childhood — at everything having a sense of wonder. Now as he stared at the albino, he felt saddened by age overtaking the great beast. At least this lone gorilla remained in the changing city. How much longer would he last, chewing on splintered pieces of wood?

He clung to this memory — to the newness of the gorilla. It was a constant in the changing landscape of the city. With his house gone, little remained to anchor

Sebastian in the environs of his childhood. Even the albino bore the weight of time on his shoulders. Sebastian wished him well in his final days of captivity. Zoos became sad places in adulthood, he noted. The last creatures of a species lived in small quarters. It must be akin to living on Mars he thought.

He exited the park and passed through a throng of protestors in the Parc Ciudad. He quickly fell in with them as they rallied outside the zoo.

A man spoke through a megaphone. "We are not caged animals. We live and breath. We should not be trapped in one place by the city. We must be free. Brothers and sisters, let's be free!"

The park was filled with people readying for a protest. They bore signs and scarves over their faces. Some spray painted the signs and nearby buildings. Others stretched their arms in anticipation of conflict. About a hundred young men and women stood while an organizer talked to the group. He rallied them with his voice. They amassed projectiles and slings in one corner, placards reading *West* in another. The smell of spray paint filled the air. The protestors bore no guns. Sebastian deduced they must be one of the more peaceful protestors — those who merely wanted to be heard. Looking at the ragged bunch now he had trouble imagining them as orderly. Even the way they gathered had the smell of anarchy about them. Shaggy beards, berets to one side, wine gourds slung, worn-out fatigues — they talked and whispered clandestinely as the man tried to organize them with assignments to different sectors of the Old Quarter.

The Old Quarter became a war ground for the dispossessed. Sebastian listened as the protestors emerged into the Placa Orwell. The Placa Orwell was a cobbled angular park frequented by junkies in the day and drunks at night. Now it was the home to protestors. The leader strode forward on the cobbled stones to a raised section in the center. "We can't live like this! Brothers, sisters disappear.

Our fathers and mothers cry at lost ones known to them. Sometimes they too fade into nothing not even recognizing us as we try to console them. There is no consolation. This is our reality — one that is fading from the face of the city. Do we sit still as our city reinvents itself, or do we rise and make our voices heard in the streets?"

A chorus of "we rise!" murmured in agreement.

"There are barriers at the Parc Ciudad and along the Promenade. These places are where we display our force. Cover the city in our signs. Fill the windows with our shouts. Don't let your family disappear in the rising skyline. Make your voices heard."

"Our voices!"

"One city! One life! One world!"

"Together we will make this city what it once was — belonging to actual people and not empty holding companies!"

Sebastian noticed two types of people in the crowd. There were the agitators — the sort to raise their fists in the air and shout. The dispossessed stood idly by — their faces registered the group's actions slowly. They sometimes chanted strings of words to no one in particular.

"You can't rise up against rebuilding the city. It's everywhere in the city. How do you repel a force that has no face?

"We will give it a face." He placed a can of spray paint in a protestor's hand who wrote *West* on a sign. The dispossessed and their forgotten family were mounting a resistance to the growth of the city. They would not stand idly by as Grey erased the skyline of the city in favor of a more commercial venture that would never cease.

"More pockets are organizing across the city," the organizer said. "They ship workers into this city like cattle! Show them that we are people. Human life cannot be valued so poorly."

Sebastian left the protestors to meet Pavel and the others.

Pavel had been taken in by some of the protestors. He expanded on his sister's situation. "Mizu is one of the dispossessed. She's lost something. Everything that mattered to her — family, home, a life — it's all been erased. She has no clue who she was. She only sees what is changing in the city. It's for people like her that we fight to be heard. They have little control. Most live lives under the care of others. After a while they can work as buskers, though you see how disconnected they are. Don't you get it Sebastian? It's class warfare."

"I'm impressed at the turnout," said Sebastian. "You think you'll make a difference this time?"

"We have to. One world. One consciousness."

*

They moved out of the Placa and back to the park where people sat about in groups relaxing in the grove. Idle chatter flitted through the air like smoke exhaled lazily, as people's passions were being awakened. As wine began to flow, faces rouged with delight. Their hearts beat faster and the drums too. Firelight emerged in the dark being twirled by entertainers.

Sebastian squirted wine into his mouth from a gourd. The red filled his mouth with tannins and fruits from the local earth. He savored the experience, trying to focus all his thought on it. In the effort he wanted to forget the pain he felt.

Some smoked hash and tobacco in conspiratorial circles. Others fortified themselves with wine squirted from skins.

One of the members of the group they joined stood up. He grasped Sebastian by the shoulder and patted him on the back. It was Rodrigo.

"I didn't think I'd see you again. For sure, I thought you were gone."

Sebastian looked at him uncomprehendingly.

"How did you get away from the cops?"

Sebastian remained silent.

"At least we're here together. Sit. You see any trace of her?"

Sebastian joined the group sitting on the ground. Some were cross-legged, others tucked their knees behind them or reclined on the lawn. They joked and laughed as the night went on. As the sun set, Rodrigo took on a more serious tone. Sebastian had trouble making people out. He heard voices from silhouetted heads, like a chorus of shadowy crows hunched on shoulders, but was not sure of who started the conspiring.

Sebastian noticed a new face, one of the dispossessed, and asked about him. "Who's this one?"

"He calls himself Che."

"That's some sick joke."

"He just sits there, cross-legged and vapid, almost drooling. Snap out of it, man!" Rodrigo smacked his cheek. Che sat still, drool collecting at the far corner of his half-open mouth.

"Hey, that's harsh. Lay off."

"You would too."

"No, I wouldn't."

"He needs to be angry. No one will make me like that. It's pathetic." Rodrigo sat down in the group's circle and pushed Che over. He rolled onto the grass like an inflatable punching bag then sat back up.

"Pathetic."

Sebastian looked to Mizu. She played with a flower she had picked outside a greenhouse at the park's entrance. It rolled in her fingers first clockwise then counter. The petals captivated her.

He inched closer to her and plucked two blades of grass from the ground. He folded them and began to weave them together. They formed a braid. He showed Mizu and she reached for it. They began to play with the vegetation and leaned onto their backs.

They kissed and talked in breathy whispers while the group smoked.

He looked about, questioning her words. The sun still washed the walk white with its rays. People still dined at tables near the greenhouse. Some children laughed as they darted about between the legs of the crowd. He thought in the air he tasted a hint of the sea, the one he had traced along the train as he rode into the city. The sea breeze rushed up from further along the promenade. Its cool touch awakened his skin. In it he could smell algae growing on stone steps, tulips in low lying fields that should have been flooded, and the London Times graced by greasy fish. In it he heard double deckers rumbling red through the streets, the wires of trolleys rattling and screeching, ringing calls to prayer from pointed minarets, and the cries of gondoliers carried across rolling waves to reach him, here. All at once he was aware of existing, of being. He became heady with sensation.

He wanted to be free.

The sun was beginning to set in the horizon over the hills. Gravel walks were embedded between lowly sloped mounds of earthen grass. The walks ran in a square pattern that expanded concentrically from a central grove of palms. Their trunks stood dreamily beyond the peaceful walks. Sebastian listened. He heard the wind passing through the fronds above. They rustled as silently as time passing. He looked at the trunks closely, his eyes wide with wonder, and the rest of the world peeled away. Only he and the palms remained. He felt the threads of their existence reverberating along with his own pulses. He knew then nothing separated them. Only the wind blew over time.

In an instant he was gone. Sebastian plunged into the palms and ran through them. Some people gathered here. Some hung about idly reclining in the shade of the palms. They drank wine casually. The sun was setting and soon this blazing oasis would come to life. A fountain could be heard trickling somewhere in the vicinity. Others still were slap tapping drums. With each tapping the sun set further. A crowd was gathering. At its center a large green expanse stretched towards more dense vegetation. Vendors who had set up tables earlier to sell necklaces and trinkets were packing their wares. An artist sat nearby carving faces into wood. As the sun fell from the horizon people were just beginning to gather. Here and there small groups had formed where drummers beat conga drums with familiarity. Their hands played hesitantly at first, brushing the skins for feeling in the night.

The rhythm had entranced him. He wanted something to overpower his thoughts, to make him feel part of a larger whole. In his life the last few days, there was nothing upon which he could take hold. Everything dissipated like mist under the morning sun. Inside he cried for such loss. His thought reached out for something solid, something tangible and lasting in life. At the moment, the sounds of the park — the drums, the chatter, the water trickling — those were the audible sounds on which he took hold.

The drums were in full effect. Earlier, people had been gathering one by one. Hawkers still stood with their handmade jewelry laid out on carpets on the ground. One or two people beat their drums tentatively in anticipation for the coming protest. Slowly a crowd grew as dusk fell upon the sky. People seemed to filter in from every direction until suddenly there was a celebration. Drummers stood in a circle around each other, pounding their palms on the dried skins. A crowd ringed them as they beat on. The pace was becoming more intense with different rhythms overlapping to form a harmonious unison. He bought some hash and rolled a joint. They smoked it together. As it passed between them, the sun set. The drum circle grew and rhythms blended together. More people began to gather. The moon rose high into the sky and suddenly night was upon the city. It arrived so lazily that people cavorted into the dark without noticing. Stars twinkled on the black canvas as a canopy to their playing. An African in the center put his pace forward. He beat on above the rest. They followed his palms accompanying his rhythm. The music bounded through the crowd. Their heads bobbed and swayed. The sound was a frenzy enrapturing dogs to chase each other around the park. People sat in groups rejoicing under the moonlight. The hum of laughter and chatter gave life to the thumps and beats vibrating through everyone.

The drums' sway urged delight. They beat faster and faster. The frenzy grew as hands slap tapped their rhythm into all of life's forms. The crowd grew with orgiastic delight. They lived for the moment, feeling its pulse. Percussion beats enlivened the streams of blood coursing through their bodies. Wine and other intoxicants aided their frenzy. Sebastian pulled Mizu aside with him and their bodies pulsed with the music.

Someone was spinning flames on the end of cords around them. They moved faster and faster around his body. Slowly they spun closer and closer to each other, until when almost in unison, the flames went out.

They kissed for what seemed hours under the moonlight, by the fountain trickling down the curves of Venus sculpted by the dreams of artisan hands. A rippling pool of radiance mirrored the starred sky above as they embraced in its shade. They separated and ran off holding hands towards the whisper of the beach rushing onto the shores of this new and ancient city.

He tried to lose himself in passion, to forget everything that had happened.

Ecstasy washed over him. Pure sensation replaced the doubts and fears that plagued him. The touch of skin against the hairs on his hand, risen slightly with heat, the breeze curling up his neck along the canals of his ears, the grass underneath depressed and warm, gravel crumpling as his feet sprawled out in the path, searching for some hold. He lost himself in the ecstatic bliss thinking only of sensation. What he felt each moment was all that mattered. Everything else receded into the abyss of what had already occurred, now already forgotten. Nothing mattered save the moment.

In the hours before morning, Sebastian left the crowd. Their cries of delight waned as he stepped out from the confines of the park. Mizu walked with him nestled around the waist by his arm. She draped hers along his shoulders, gently caressing the muscles on his back. He felt enlivened and exhausted at the same time. With an effort he moved his feet forward, eyes drooping with the heavy night. The sun would rise in a few short hours. Still, the sights and sounds of the night boiled within him. He looked on things with a new appreciation, one he hadn't found since his first days in the Americas. The feeling exhilarated him.

"You're looking for an aleph, right? I can show you one."

"An aleph?"

"They exist. Weren't you looking for one? It's time. I'll show you."

5

They left the group and threaded their way into the streets of the Old Quarter. Light streamed down from above the rooftops. The dissenters busied themselves with sign making and armed themselves for the coming protest. Mizu, Sebastian, and Pavel picked their way along an alley through a board covering a hole in one of the buildings. The entrances were hidden to these buildings, but none had locks, just a secret to the way in.

Light crept in from around the boarded up windows of the house they entered. The place must have been a derelict building in the Old Quarter. The pathways taken underground rose into the world above where citizens abandoned houses. A gathering occurred in the room adjacent to the subterranean entrance.

Sebastian picked his footing carefully between buildings. They walked in an abandoned theater. Refuse filled the aisles. It looked as if squatters had spent the last few months here, though none could be seen apart from Sebastian's group. He looked at the stage. Mizu stood atop it and pulled a hatch open in its center.

"Through here."

The dispossessed, as Sebastian saw them, lacked order. The squatters who rallied against police were one aspect of the movement. They occupied buildings in an attempt to reclaim what was lost. Often these buildings were decrepit, forgotten places. By reclaiming it, the squatters mocked the properties being erected and gave themselves homes in the midst of a city that no longer wanted them. These were the sort to smash bottles at the police station. They were the brothers and sisters, the sons and daughters of the dispossessed. Their rage could be vented forcibly in the street.

The dispossessed acted differently. They lacked the intensity of emotion, the rage others felt. The dispossessed moved in an eerie unison. They all moved as if they were on display all the time. Their movements were slow and clouded as if they had no clear idea of what transpired, yet when asked about their circumstances they often could reply with unsettling acumen. Theirs was a lot that accepted no privacy. Everything was on display. Sebastian thought them the living dead. Zombies without a home. Such was the price they paid to be on display. They had all seen the aleph and their lives were forever changed for it.

"What about the aleph?"

Pavel spoke. "I've seen things. Places that don't exist. Places that do exist. They are becoming less and less. You no longer see any and all places. Place is so particular. Place changes so fast. The aleph shows emptiness. The places you do see, they're images from the past. Sometimes the images are all that remains as ghosts of the Old Quarter. The images in the aleph haunt our reality.

"With the movement we can work toward integrating what the aleph shows and what is in our memory. Collectively we should be able to restore the city. It exists, still, in our imaginations. Everyone must get involved though. The dispossessed need a voice in order to return to this world. *West* is that voice."

"He's wrong, you know, about *West*." Mizu said to Sebastian in a low whisper. "*West* isn't a voice for the missing. It's something else — something you feel. It's like the wind shifting."

They entered a room guarded by two protestors. A man inside who looked like their leader ushered them in.

"The aleph. Show them the aleph." The dispossessed uttered this last.

The leader stepped forward. "Come with me."

Mizu took Sebastian and Pavel to see the aleph.

The man spoke as he guided them deeper into the midst of dissenters. "People need to become aware of the collective consciousness movement. The missing need a voice. That voice is *West*. It's everywhere in the city. We all are *West*. Get with it. One consciousness, one existence. It's all of us. Its unity, man. One world."

"For real. One world. One consciousness."

A room stood before them with no furniture, though it was lined by people standing or squatting against the four walls. They looked hungry and smoked tensely. No light crept in through the windows, which were shuttered tight. Sebastian walked to the center of the room and held forth his hands.

"One world. One consciousness." They chanted around the room.

A blue ball of energy formed in his palm. It seemed to emerge from his veins, as if it pulsed with the blood inside him, though it formed like a magnetic gel he gathered with outstretched fingers. Sebastian felt it radiating in his palm. The vitality coursed through him. His skin illuminated white by the ball of energy. It grew from the size of a marble to fill his palm, hovering just a few centimeters from the matter of his hand.

Sebastian saw places, just like with the twins. The Promenade. The Parc Ciudad. Placa Orwell. The hills surrounding the city. A church overlooking the hills and the streets leading up them. He stood on a hilltop surveying all the land the city covered trying to picture it as one entity. All of it flitted past the small surface of the aleph straight into his thoughts. He saw the whole of the city in this blue ball of energy before him.

*

"You have to choose. Choose whether to believe or not," said Mizu. "Choose whether you see the past or the future. Either these places exist or they don't."

"It's a mirage," Rodrigo said as he stepped from the wall. "Come on. You can't believe this. It's just a trick. This thing only glows. You don't see anything. It has no real power."

"He doesn't believe."

"You bet I don't believe. I believe in these." He held his arms forth, fists at the end. These will change the world, not glow sticks."

When Sebastian stood back, when the visions had passed, then he understood. The agitators understood the history of what they saw. They saw only loss among the images of the aleph. That was why they felt such anger at the city and those who changed its surface. The dispossessed no longer saw this history. The aleph left them vacant. It erased thoughts from the mind but did not replace them with anything substantive. The remainder of Sebastian's thoughts were malleable and impressionable. The city had yet to shape their minds as clay could be molded by hands. Sebastian understood how the group was divided. Throughout, he clung to the image of his house in disrepair. He clung to his father's words in the journal. He clung to his memory of Julía. These images kept him sane in the juxtaposition of places he saw in the aleph.

"An aleph formed by chi energy. This is what Arturo wants. This is what my father was after."

"This is how you channel souls."

The blue ball vanished shortly after these words. The members of the room all remained silent. They observed the passing of the aleph.

"It changes places. Never stays in one place for long. Once it moves we have to find it again, but it knows where we are. It draws us to it. It wants to be seen by us alone. Already I can feel it."

Voices came from the throng surrounding Sebastian at the walls of the room.

"Elana disappeared too. When will it end?"

"You'd think that we've been pushed down enough. Why do they keep doing this?"

"Because they can. You would if you had the power."

"We need to do something. We can't let them keep pushing us down like this."

"The aleph is calling."

"Where else can we go?"

"Listen to her. We'll find it again."

"The worst thing is people think they are free. They slave away for the people who drive up the costs of their lives. And they're thankful to be given their money back, only to funnel it back into the system."

"Lunacy, man."

"We should fight them. Stage an uprising. I'm tired of running."

"Run to the aleph."

"Yeah, but how do you find them? They're faceless. No one takes the blame. The conspiracy has spread too far. People don't even know when they are involved.

"I know who's behind it. All of it. The missing people. The changing city. We can get him." Sebastian realized he had said the last. "He's unveiling a new building. The opening ceremony is later this week. I can show you where."

"We can take him out."

"We can put a face to our loss."

"Use the aleph to stop them. It has the power, I know it."

"I just want my family back."

"This violence will never end."

"Let's do it."

6

He came to in front of Xavi's body.

It was daytime, the afternoon. The body lay in one of the narrow, angled streets. The man's throat was slit. The blood poured out onto the street. It ran through the channels of stone flooding the construction dust that accumulated. In a patchwork pattern it spread across the grid until the blood cascaded down through a rusty metal grate into the sewers below.

The body belonged to Xavi. There were many reasons the man should be dead. Sebastian alone had more than one. It seemed like everyone in this city was disappearing one by one. Soon the only ones left would be the buildings. Empty, hollow, corroded like the ruins of ancient civilizations about which no one remembers anything.

Sebastian felt a pang of regret for leaving Xavi with Grey. They had plans for Xavi and Sebastian doubted he would benefit from them. If only Xavi had been forthright to begin with, Sebastian could have helped.

He had lost time again. Now Xavi was gone. He thought again to his house being dismantled. He missed his mother. He wished he could talk to her now. She would know what to say to him to calm him down. These instances of lost time had to stop. He could not go on living his life when he could not account for missing sections. It was exasperating when he tried so hard to keep it together amid all the chaos in the city.

Sebastian regretted that he did not have the chance to talk to Xavi further. The city seemed to push everyone who had plans for it out of the way. You either moved to its rhythm or were spit out like Xavi.

Sebastian saw the crowds of pedestrians plodding at the opening to the alley. The light shined brightly out there, not like in the confines of the alleys of the Old Quarter.

Shopping bags shimmered with their brisk pace. Sebastian returned to Xavi. He searched his pockets, careful that no one looked down the alley. It was probably too dark between the overlapping buildings to be seen, but Sebastian felt he should be prudent. There was nothing in his pockets, not even his wallet or ID. Xavi was to become another of the faceless, lost to the world, and no one would care but Sebastian. He looked into his friend's face one last time before returning to the stream of people scurrying past in the sun.

Next to him, in the street, stood a woman. She stood painting the wall of a building. "Everyone knows everything. At least they think they do. There are connections everywhere to everything. Time makes a monkey of us all."

Her arms went up, then down in long strokes that bent slowly at the wrist. First up, then down with a flourish at the wrist where her fingers held the brush. Each individual hair leaving paint on the wall next to Xavi's body. She worked as if entranced, neither looking at nor acknowledging Sebastian as she painted.

"The days are long. They never end."

"How long have I been here?"

"The days are long. They never end."

"Who are you?"

"Does anyone know anyone? You just appeared like a vision of palms in the distance."

"What?"

"Palms. In the distance. A mirage like an oasis."

"Why are you painting?"

Her hand went up then down in a decisive stroke. "I just am."

She finished a few strokes until the word *West* read on the wall.

"Who are you?"

"I'm Mizu. There's a man on the ground next to you."

Sebastian wrung his hands. "We need to leave." The light still shone on her shoulders as she stepped back to observe Sebastian and the corpse.

"Did you kill him?"

"No, I didn't kill him. Let's go before someone finds him." He ushered her back from the painting and began brusquely walking through the Old Quarter.

"I don't now what's real anymore. The lights, the color, they sparkle in the distance. People talk but I have no idea what they say. Even you talk nonsense. I shift in and out of time, catching words as they fly from people's mouths, finding myself in one place then another."

"What are you saying? Now isn't the time for nonsense. Xavi's dead."

"There's no distinction between waking and dreaming life."

"Stop talking or I'll begin to think you killed him."

"It's possible. This happens sometimes. Lost time."

Sebastian walked with his head tilted to one side as if an invisible leash dragged him along the street. He would walk in circles to sit down coiling the invisible line. His inner ear throbbed.

What's happening to me, he thought. The last he remembered he had just seen the aleph in the old theater. Next he stood in the street where Mizu painted a wall next to Xavi's body.

As he navigated away from the body, he noticed people marched naked in the streets, not in a streak of freedom but catatonic, as if they had no idea what they did. Was this the protest they planned? He moved between them as they marched slowly plodding forward like animated mannequins come to life. They dotted the streets of the Old Quarter. Their minds were so foggy they had forgotten to wear clothes. He hoped naked people were not a sign of things to come. Maybe Arturo was right. They are a lost generation — lost in time. Could that be where they are right now, Sebastian thought, some other time? He felt his sanity leaving him. With so many odd sights, he was beginning to lose his grip.

Mizu pulled him along. "This way. It's the aleph. I feel it."

They threaded their way toward the aleph as agitators prepared for a clash with the police in the city. The dispossessed marched lost in the streets. Mizu seemed more composed than she was at the park. Sebastian noted that the dispossessed must go through phases, like a metamorphosis of sorts. Some of the time they spoke in riddles. Other times they were more astute. Were they phases in a cycle of growth? Mizu had shown him moments of clarity. The aleph awakened her insights. Still, she might not be far off from acting like the mannequins in the street. If this was protest Sebastian pictured similar scenes all over the city. They marched toward the Expansion baring all. Perhaps that was the point. They showed their vulnerability to the world. Sebastian stopped to look closely at one. It stared vacantly ahead. No register appeared in its eyes.

They're someplace else, Sebastian surmised. Mizu tugged him along through the bodies faster from his inquiry.

"We're almost there."

A policeman took notice of the two from the corner of the street.

Sebastian noticed a knife in his own hand. It dripped onto the street. Had he taken it from Xavi's body? He couldn't be sure. So much of the world seemed unhinged. He dipped into a side alley with Mizu, avoiding the policeman's stare at the naked mannequins.

The doctor's office was nearby in the Old Quarter. He wondered at how he had come to the opposite end of the Old Quarter. He had no memories of the time between being at the Park Ciudad and finding Xavi. He decided to get help from the doctor's office. Maybe the doctor could help him with his recent memory loss. Mizu too seemed like she could benefit from a consultation. Sebastian had no idea what would prompt her back to herself. Maybe this was her new self. This was the person Sebastian would know. She had been like this for a few months according to Pavel. It was possible she was beyond help. Still, the naked mannequins unsettled Sebastian. He wanted to get off the streets.

*

Loose, mostly crumpled and balled up paper filled the floor of the office. A lone cat patrolled the reception area. The remaining chairs were broken, as if someone had kicked them in two. Several chairs were scattered in the tumble of papers at the entryway. When he ventured further within the doctor's office, he found an old cot and a folding lamp, nothing resembling a doctor's office. Even here, he thought. The reconstruction took the doctor.

Why had he left? He was the only man with any clue as to what was happening in the city. He wondered if the man was actually a doctor or some charlatan hawking cheap fixes to gullible people like himself. He searched frantically through the mess for some clue. He retrieved one from the floor. On its face showed an invoice for service, another a flyer for luxury lofts. All the invoices were the same. *West* read over the patient names on the lined papers. Sebastian started to gather them together. Mizu kicked a few as she walked haphazardly.

"What are you doing?"

"All the names. I have to have them. All the names of all the people he treated. No one will forget them."

"Silly."

They descended past the broken elevator to the street where Inspector Torres accosted him in the alley.

"I thought I told you. You know better than this."

The skin around the inspector's eyes was drawn tightly around his face. He looked as if he hadn't slept in days. Too many looked like that in Sebastian's mind. "He's gone. The doctor's gone."

"He moved out along with his stupid solution. There's no place in this city for pranksters like him. No place can bring them back once they're gone."

Sebastian saw the set jaw of a city man, not the sympathetic father he met earlier in his return to the city. He wouldn't find any solace with him. Sebastian noticed paint on his own fingers from a spray can and decided to change tack.

"How is your daughter?"

"Time makes a monkey of us all. You'll see."

"What?"

"Ignore her, Torres. You've seen the people in the streets. Your daughter, they have no idea what they're doing."

"Don't mention her in the same sentence as these rats. She had faith. She believed in something." He gripped Sebastian by his collar. "Can you say the same? Can you? Do you believe in anything or is it all rubbish?"

Sebastian shoved him off. "Lay off. I looked for my father. Julía too. I believe in looking for an answer. Not like you. You gave up."

"That's it. You're coming in with me." The Inspector grabbed Sebastian by the arm and shoved him up against the wall. "You could have saved her. All you had to do was leave."

"Julía's out there somewhere. Her I'll find, no matter what you do. You won't stop it. No one will. It's too big for you."

The Inspector frisked Sebastian and found the knife in his sock. "What's this? No need for a knife where you're going." He leaned in and whispered in Sebastian's ear. "You're no better then the rest. You hear me?"

Sebastian threw his head back and knocked the Inspector's nose. Blood poured down his weary face. "Run!" Sebastian yelled at Mizu.

The two took to the streets trying to escape while the Inspector stood dazed. Sebastian looked over his shoulder and saw Inspector Torres clutching his red nose. Torres found a curb and dropped his weight down. He must be exhausted by his search, Sebastian thought. The man is collapsing, inside and out. Not me, he thought, not me.

7

They had taken to the streets now. Everywhere Sebastian went, the Old Quarter protestors screamed and shook their hands in the air. They mounted a small resistance against the change occurring in their city. The dispossessed too could be found at every corner, lost in the warren of the Old Quarter.

Arturo's skinny frame picked its way through the waves of rioters in the Old Quarter. He angled sideways through the flow of people yelling with their fists in the air. They moved in clusters, making their way to meet riot police at the placa. Individuals stopped to spray *West* on the dun colored buildings. The Old Quarter brimmed with protest from the arms of its streets crossing the land of the city.

In the midst of his flight from the police, Sebastian singled out Arturo as he threaded a wave of rioters who shook Arturo as they ran past. He's heading for the aleph, thought Sebastian. The Museo was not far and the building housing the aleph Arturo found was nearby. Sebastian yelled at him across the street. Arturo struggled with a few rioters who ran past, toward the placa where most of the demonstrators met with the opposition.

"That won't work forever. I saw a police station attacked. They're everywhere now."

"Those are the few misguided radicals. They're not the norm. Most just want to feel someone understands. It's a way of moving the disenfranchised. If they find a voice, they are less likely to be in conflict with our interests. We're filtering them like wind through the appropriate channels. They go where we want them — away from our progress.

"It's like Gogol's Dead Souls. We're collecting intangible pieces of culture. The city is literally being rebuilt from the ground up. Someone has to collect all the spiritual energy being released. I've found a way to store it. Your father knew an aleph existed in the city. That's what he was looking for."

"It drove him crazy. You can't be a part of this. They won't welcome you."

"Yes. He was consumed by it. I have more robust means at my disposal though. I can handle the stress through my network of informants. They see the value in an inside man."

"With so many people aware of what you're doing, why didn't anyone know what happened to my father?"

"People knew. They just didn't care to tell you. There was nothing for them to profit from. That's why I told you. The uninitiated have a price to pay. Yours is finding the aleph. Your father wanted it. If you want him you need to find an aleph in the city. Something concrete."

Grey's man had told him the last of his father's work was somewhere near here. Sebastian walked past the teenagers smoking in the plaza and looked into one of the passageways leading to where he stood. It was a small, cobbled street that appeared to lead off to nowhere in particular. He doubted that this angled path through squat white buildings would lead to a site of grand proportions. He tried another of the entranceways to the square and met the same. Another and another appeared to him as he paced along all sides of the plaza. The place had become a labyrinth to him. He decided he should retrace his steps in order. A new perspective would help him find his way, yet as he stepped from the threshold of the plaza, he found his footing unsure. The path he had chosen seemed no different to him than the ones he had observed before. His mind was uncertain of which entrance he had come from.

He had known this area well at one point. Now his steps were faltering. Surely, he thought, he must be able to recognize some structure, some landmark, even in construction, to guide him from this prison. He scanned the horizon franticly. No spire, no tower, no light greeted his gaze. His hopes of freedom disappeared as night blanketed the remnants of the day. The horizon was dark and unrecognizable. Sebastian stood, feebly trying to retrace his steps, but in vain. His memory had failed. The city surrounding him was strange and foreign. He had no idea where to go or even where he stood at the moment. Even if Sebastian did remember the first street, there would be another, and another after that which he must traverse to get to his final destination. A small siege of panic seized him.

"The aleph … I have to see it," Arturo said as he guided them to the site.

"Get a hold of yourself."

"No! It's real. All this time I've been searching for it and these rioters know where it is. They've been hiding it from me. I have to see it. I can't lose it now, not after it's shown me so much."

Blue paint smeared the edge of his suit jacket. He ran, frantic, with the tide of rioters. His skinny frame shook with terror as they hindered his movement. Sebastian edged closer.

Police advanced from the opposite end of the street in the warren of the Old Quarter. They bore riot gear — large shields and helmets and guns that shot bean bags. Sebastian grabbed Arturo by the arm. "They're going to take you. In this rush, there's no good or bad, just people in the way. You'll be taken." A canister of tear gas rattled ahead of them spewing smoke on the rioters. They began coughing and doubled over. Others pulled bandanas over their mouths but their eyes still turned red and watery.

"In here," a voice urged them.

"They ducked into a building where an old man ushered them in. He pulled a carpet from the floor to reveal a hatch leading to a cellar.

As the hatch fell open he said, "Quickly we must escape from here."

Mizu, Sebastian, Arturo and the old man descended into the space below street level down the stairs of the cellar. The old man pulled the hatch shut behind them and light reduced to a few streams edging through the wood above. He lit a lantern and a room appeared in the darkness below the Old Quarter. The old man took care to avert his eyes from the center of the room.

"This is it. The key to all places," the old man said

"You're not going to trick anyone again, Arturo."

"No! I promise you it's more real than the riot outside. It's the key to developing lasting life in the city."

The old man stepped toward them. "The aleph is a mystery. All who see it must endeavor a journey of their own. Some see singularities, others the whole of the city."

"Unbelievable. Who are you?"

"Just an old man."

Arturo crowded close to the aleph in the center of the room. Sebastian looked to the old man. He averted his gaze from Arturo who in the center advanced on the blue glow of the aleph. The old man held the lantern aloft with one arm and a grimace bore on his face. He seemed to regret something about the place but Sebastian could not tell what. Arturo's eyes lit up reflecting the glow of the aleph. Scenes of the city lit up Arturo's irises. Havoc spread through the Old Quarter. The streets emptied rioters into police. The tumult grew over the land. The hills surrounding the city appeared peaceful on Arturo's eyes. The Expansion's broad avenues were clogged with police vans and blockades. The broad avenues and rectangular blocks flitted past. Arturo could not move his hands from the sides of the aleph; a few inches from his palms the glow filled the room. The old man ushered them to a side passageway with the lantern in hand. Arturo did not move. He did not hear any of them any more.

"It takes another," the old man said.

Sebastian tried to pull Arturo free but Arturo didn't budge from the spot. He was attached to the glow filling the room. In the center the aleph showed the city to Arturo — a slave to its viewing glory.

"Leave him. There's nothing we can do for him now. We have more to do before this cell is compromised." The old man led the way into the side passageway. Sebastian and Mizu followed the light of the lantern as he spoke. The man was too quick for Sebastian to gain sight of his face.

His voice rattled back to Sebastian between the woodwork of the passage. "The aleph changes places. It appears and disappears depending on who needs to see it. There is no set place, though it appears in cellars underground more often than the light of day."

As they edged through the passageway, Sebastian could see through the wooden boards into the streets. Rioters with scarves over their noses and mouths slung rocks. Their eyes fervid with power, they flitted in and out of sight.

The old man could have been his father, or another man who aped him from the same experiences. Sebastian could not believe that he would encounter an exact — so similar save for a few external appearances. The man looked exactly as his father would, if he had been relegated to a life working in the streets of the city. He had a disheveled, worn aura about him, as if he had been a street vendor for thirty years and knew all the local comings and goings.

The man smacked his lips together several times slowly as if the whole of his mouth stuck when closed. After a minute or so he seemed satisfied and looked directly at Sebastian. He spoke, tilting his chin up, looking to Sebastian, and his words came out of a ragged throat but bore directly into Sebastian.

"Why are you here?"

"It's you. What happened? I don't really know."

"I don't know. I don't know. No one knows."

"How long have they left you here?"

The man scratched his chin. "Not sure. Hard to measure time."

"I need to get out of here. This was stupid. The whole thing, stupid."

"What's waiting for you?"

"Nothing, really."

"Then why hurry?"

"I don't want to live my life in a tunnel underground."

"There are worse things."

Sebastian paused. "And what do you know, old man?"

"I think you have nothing. Everyone has nothing. No one realizes it until the end."

"Unless you can find a way out, I don't want to hear it."

"Here, I'll show you what I've done." The man pulled the grate away. Sebastian approached and saw a small tunnel that had been hidden by the grate.

Across the walls, the man had sketched the city skyline, only this one was familiar to Sebastian. It did not show the buildings under construction, or the ones built in his absence. It was the skyline he recognized, one from his youth. The chalk structures ran on all sides of the room, so Sebastian could turn in a 360° fashion to imagine being in a city of the past, buried deep underground. The details were so explicit as to have windows and cornices on all of the buildings. The sight amazed Sebastian. Such an intricate knowledge of the city capable of reproducing its smallest details through memory, was astounding.

"Xavi knows. He's seen it. He can tell you what it means."

The latch to the outside door sounded. A wheel spun, opening the lock. The heavy bulk of the door slid in its track. Light from a flashlight broke the darkness.

"Who are you talking to?"

It was Pavel. "There's an old man in here."

Pavel flicked a switch on the wall and fluorescent lights flickered on overhead. Humming rebounded on the walls as Sebastian's eyes adjusted. Street signs and tags covered the room, one tag overlapping another. An old ticket counter stood on one side. The floor tiles were cracked and dented into the ground. In a few places you could see earth underneath and moss growing on the tiles. Spider webs hung in the corners in long strands bundled together like curtains.

One read 'IF GRAFFITI CHANGED ANYTHING IT WOULD BE ILLEGAL.' Another showed a colorful childlike drawing in what looked like crayon of a house with a stenciled man hammering black and white boards across the door. A little girl watched sadly. Charlie Brown smoked a cigarette and tilted a can of gasoline. A man in a black and white suit, a fedora and a suitcase wore a sign reading '0% INTEREST IN PEOPLE.' Another, the house of parliament filled with monkeys in suits.

The old man sat huddled in the crease between the wall and floor. It looked as if he lived there, nestled on top of a worn piece of cardboard stained with dirt. He wore a straggly white beard and ratty clothes. He had an arm raised over his eyes, shielding him from the fluorescent lights above. "Can't think with these lights. Off! Turn 'em off!"

Sebastian looked down. In his fingers he grasped a page the man gave to him. He held it before him and saw the familiar spidery crawl drawn across the page.

I passed the cathedral St. Jaumé. Graffiti covered its wall as I passed along the side toward the house. The man painting it stood still, waving a can of spray paint in front of him. He told me he wrote love letters, all over the city. It was his art — letters in pictures strewn across the city in the hope of finding the one he loved. He had no idea where she was. All he could do was paint messages for her to find, hoping she would come back. I imagine chocolates or flowers more appropriate for a woman but there was something novel in his thoughts. I looked at the cathedral differently afterward. It's as if the mold from which the building was made had been broken. Other buildings, I noticed as well. They too seemed different, like some new homogenized plates acting as the model for new growth. The street artist added a layer of depth to the iterations of buildings appearing all over the city. The average person on the street sees no relief in faceless mannequins. Street art is vandalism, clouding the shiny exterior world of storefronts. Everything is on display, even at churches. I can't reconcile that people accept these images, these models as representational of the human experience. Something is being lost in the copying of styles. There is no soul to these creations popping up in the city; but a man writing love letters in paint, there is soul. These new buildings are run off of the same plate, one after another, identical for all extensive purposes. None of them know how to create a plate anymore. They cannot etch anything, much more so a plate. In this, something is lost. Fire has gone out of the minds of the faceless souls now dwelling in this city. Soon everything will be extinguished. The city will walk blankly, seeing and absorbing nothing. I fear for my soul as these apparitions occur more and more often. Everywhere I go they haunt me. Still, I must endure. I must create something lasting. If I didn't write lover letters from paint cans on walls, who will? I will make buildings that are art and in these structures people will feel a stirring in their souls. The street artist inspired me. I had almost forgotten how to live until I saw his passionate act of vandalism. That is where true art and love will survive in this city.

I met Grey on the site today. I told him I wouldn't work on the project anymore, not with its current design. He asked me to stay but I told him I had to change everything. This vexed him. He complained about building schedules and extra costs but I ignored him. I retreated to the house, deciding not to visit the site again until I had a plan. I spend my days now drafting and redrafting what the city should look like. It's elusive, my vision. Every time I draw near, something isn't right and I have to redo the whole plan. I feel invigorated, more so than I have in months.

*

Sebastian bent over to look more closely at the man. "Just who are you?"

The man mumbled to himself and mashed his lips together before puckering his face and looking up at Sebastian.

The resemblance was there, distant but existent. In the wide, crazed eyes of this vagrant Sebastian saw the likeness of his father. The man's hair was long and straggly and his beard unkempt but Sebastian thought he could make the outline of his father's bone structure in the cheeks and nose. "What's your name?"

"Name? Don't have one. No use for it anymore. What's in a name?" The old man lost himself in laughter at the last bit.

Sebastian held the paper before him, gripping it tightly and crumpling the page. "Where did you find this writing?"

The vagrant rolled over, turning his back to them. He pulled a spread sheet of newsprint over his body. "Trash. People tossed it. No need for it anymore. No one reads."

It can't be him. These words turned over again and again in Sebastian's mind. The picture of the man in rags, hair long and greasy, beard unkempt, was nothing like the image he held of his father. His father was an upright man, tall and intimidating. He had run as much from him as anything else in the city. This quivering mess of a vagrant could not be the ordered and disciplined man who had crippled his mother emotionally. Sebastian had refused to inherit the same fate, but now, confronted with a distorted image of the man he rejected, he wondered what it was he really ran from.

*

They emerged from the passageways in old buildings hiding the aleph onto a walkway that ran perpendicular to the passage. Above, ran a boardwalk. Before them, cement slabs met the sand. A few cardboard shanties had been erected by the homeless. Two played dominos as the torrent raged on in the Old Quarter. Extra panels were stacked in a wire frame grocery cart nearby.

The old man walked dreamlike along the shore. Sebastian had been trying to gain a clear view of him since they entered the passage. The man's feet pressed lightly into the sand, toes depressing sand. The imprints disappeared as he stepped forward. It was as if he were some ghost unable to leave a permanent impact on the world.

The waves washed ashore, foamy at its outer reaches. The water dragged back across the wet sand to retreat out to sea. It seemingly did not touch the man's legs, just washed right through them. Sebastian could not avert his eyes. The scene transfixed him. Further out on the water, the moon dappled on the waves. The light shimmered with a luminous glow creating a serenely illuminated seascape. Sebastian was amazed that the lights from the city weren't reflected on the water. It was as if they ceased to exist in this moment in time. For once since his return, he felt peace. His legs stepped toward the water. He had not made them move. They moved on their own, as if pulled by some silent siren song delivered as the waves washed ashore. Closer he came, toward the man, his double father, treading along the surf. His feet stopped. The surf washed in, dowsing his pant legs. The double stepped past, leaving no trace on the beach.

"What are you?"

"Don't you know by now?"

182

The man kept plodding along. He spoke, but his head did not turn to acknowledge Sebastian.

"It's impossible. You can't ... you can't be him. He's dead."

"No one told you. They never saw him dead. He just left."

Sebastian paused to consider the man's words then hurried after him. "Everyone's leaving this city. Everyone's disappearing. Tell me why."

"This city is changing. There's not room for everyone in it."

"How could you have let this happen?"

"I didn't have a say in it."

"The city won't let me go. I've tried. I left it behind but it keeps wanting me. It will suffocate me if I don't get out."

"You're just like the others. Nothing special about you, no matter what you think. No one can escape the past. You'll end up like me, alone and forgotten. I'm forced to walk the shore and streets of this city until I find peace. That day could be a long way off."

Sebastian splashed forward, his legs knee deep in the water.

"But why? What makes you keep going?"

"There's noting else to do. Stop running."

"Don't you remember?"

The churn of hoary waves filled Sebastian's ears. Nothing else could be heard, even as the man continued on. Sebastian stood breathless from the scene. He could not move any more. No words came to his mouth. He was transfixed by the man and the landscape. He felt the coolness of the sea rush past the palms of his hands hanging limply by his side. The sensation was a real and tangible one. He felt just as others would. No dream could produce the chill in his fingertips but here he was amazed by what he had seen.

At the end of their conversation the man continued on as he had been, plodding forward in the surf, leaving no trace of his passing behind him. It was erased by the sea. Sebastian watched him for as long as he could, the man becoming a distant speck along the beach that he could not distinguish from the rectangular pylons of piers and small square buildings on the shore.

"Why don't you remember me?" He turned back to Mizu. "What did they do to him? Why can't he remember?"

Mizu stood up from her perch on the rock jetty. She had a far off and distant stare as she spoke, her eyes transfixed by the stars shimmering on the sea. "No one does. They choose to forget. It's easier than remembering everything they've lost."

"Is that what you did? Is that why you are the way you are?"

"You make it sound like I had a choice."

Mizu gathered her things from the beach and made to leave. Sebastian couldn't leave yet. He could not accept the fates that befell his father and Julía. Maybe there was no choice for them, he thought. Maybe all you could do was keep living, keep looking forward. His eyes sought out the horizon where the sea met the night sky. The line was distant, across a churning mass that met the airy firmament above — so open and full of possibility. Sebastian wondered at the tides and the gravitational pull moving bodies of water. He too felt under the moon's pull. He felt torn by the forces around him, like, Julía, like his father.

How long will I last, he wondered. How long until I end up like them — ghosts of what they once were, shells of their previous selves? Already he had noticed the changes in his reports. Gaps in his memory increased. After meeting with Grey at the port, that's when things started. The meeting was the first time he began to understand the phenomena of the city. In that same instant, he began to lose his cognizance. Mizu placed her arm around him and they walked along the shore in the wake of his father trying to appreciate the beauty of the night sky.

His world did not make sense anymore. Everything was so different. What should have been familiar was unrecognizable. Even stranger, the exotic newness of the place felt familiar to him. He had no idea which feeling to trust and found himself following the man. Sebastian wandered through narrow alleys barely wide enough for two. They zigzagged around the buildings behind which they had formed. Sometimes a path stared directly into the next building, offering no exit until he was at the end and saw another narrow alley leading off perpendicular. People slept in some of the turns. Sebastian stumbled over them. Their bodies were hidden in the shadow. Holes in some of the building walks allowed glimpses of people congregating in these abandoned buildings. They were okupas — squatters who occupied the vacant figures of the city. Sebastian realized that he had no place to go. His home had been deconstructed. He settled into a space away from the conspiratorial words of the okupas. His home was now in a forgotten corner of the city in a derelict building. Such were the realities of existence for Sebastian as he waited for sleep to come and wash his thoughts from him.

8

He lost time again. Like at the base of the statue, he found himself in a strange environment with no recollection of how he came there. He found himself in a crowd gathered in front of a new building. The old man was gone. Mizu too. The crowd looked half-interested. A few press members stood near the front cameras, ready. Others walked past the gathering, not noticing. Days must have passed. Would this gathering be as fraught as the rioters in the previous days?

In the square, people stood shoulder to shoulder. The hum of conversation vibrated in the air, giving Sebastian the impression of walking on a wire that twitched with his weight on one foot. His eyes darted about warily, searching for some sign of what was to come, but no one could be picked out from the crowd. It was a uniform mass with a life its own. All he could do was listen and be ready when its pulse quickened.

The sun beat down hard on them. Sebastian felt his neck roasting to a deep red. Sweat rolled down his temples and he wiped them clean. Others dabbed at rivulets too running down their necks, along spines, and below eyes.

At the broad end of the square, a stage was set. It stood before a shiny new wall of glass windows that was the front of a new commerce building.

Grey stepped onto the stage and began a speech prepared in advance.

"Our community has been growing so prosperously that it's hard to keep up with progress. I stand here today to open another of our works, another building constructed by people who envision not what this city is, but what it can be. It makes me proud to say that this building is customized to meet the needs of the city. These needs are great, and it requires great men to meet them." Scant applause came from his peers onstage and a few in the crowd. The crowd looked to be getting more agitated by the moment. Sebastian wondered how long they would listen, enthralled by Grey. "In what I hope to be a vision of things to come, we have created this new part of the city's skyline. Hopefully, people will look to it with adoration for what the city can become, and not what it has been. We shall not look to the past as we move forward, but to the future and all the things that we can become."

"What about the people? Where are the missing?" a crowd member shouted.

Grey continued. "We can't concern ourselves with those that become lost. There are too many opportunities to keep track of."

"Your opportunities are arrest records!"

Grey placed his hands calmly on the podium. "Contractors cannot be held responsible for the actions of the few. We are a positive effect on the local community. We provide jobs and new energy to the Old Quarter."

Sebastian spotted Rodrigo and Pavel in the crowd. If they were here, things would not stay calm for long. He could not imagine them listening to Grey for long. Rodrigo made eye contact with Sebastian. He nodded toward the stage.

Sebastian couldn't stand Grey's hypocrisy. The man was behind so much of the turmoil in the city. A protestor pushed his way to the front of the crowd and climbed on stage. "This has to stop. No more!" Security convened around him and made to arrest him.

People slowly gathered. One by one they stopped to watch, intrigued by this one man's struggle. His efforts seemed juvenile, to confront a vastly superior force. There was no hope for him. One guard held his forearm against the back of the protestor's head. The other curled under his neck, choking him. More security grappled with his limbs, trying to take him down.

The faces of those who stopped seemed permanently frozen at first. They did not register events, merely stared vacantly at the spectacle. Stopping in itself was an achievement for them, Sebastian thought. Once they were pulled from the crowd bustling past, the opportunity to reflect presented itself. Merely by witnessing, they broke the thrall of the passerby.

Eventually, they drew nearer the conflict. One man clutching a briefcase stepped closer to security. They warned him back but he kept advancing. Others too began to thaw. They moved toward the conflict, escalating. Now security brandished batons and pushed back advancing onlookers.

A cry rang out. "You can't treat us like that!" The man with the briefcase jostled with a guard; his hand clutched a baton pushing him back. "I'm a person too."

One by one they drew nearer, slowly awakening to the reality surrounding them. They began to swarm. They found a voice. They began to protest.

"I'm a person, not a user profile."

One man pulled a bottle off the ground and hurled it at the stage.

Others joined the fray. From all directions, projectiles flew in the air — bottles, fruit, signs. The stage became under assault, others acting like vandals in the crowd.

Sebastian escaped in the fray, pulled a bandana up over his nose and hurled a bottle over the crowd at the stage. It hit the podium and shattered. The men onstage ducked in reaction. Security guards moved in front of them and pulled each aside. The unveiling of the new building was postponed. The crowd began to jostle each other. Some pushed forward raising their hands and shouting. Others threaded backward, away from the chaos beginning to ensue. Photographers clicked buttons on their cameras as more debris and refuse were thrown. Social media bloggers held their phones in front of them, narrating the events they filmed. On the distant electronics store, their coverage aired in the windows full of televisions after uploading.

The police dispatched in riot gear — shields before them, helmets with clear face masks. Some shot canisters of tear gas into clusters close to the stage. Others were tazed. Sebastian saw the riot guard advancing and made his way into one of the alleys.

Sebastian saw Rodrigo shot in the chest with a beanbag. He fell and police moved in with batons around him and began clubbing his prostrate body. Jordi, the leader from the Placa Orwell, screamed as he tried to wipe pepper spray from his eyes. Sebastian lost sight of Pavel. He fell in the square and was most likely trampled by the crowds stampeding in all directions.

Sebastian fled.

They knew. They knew something had been planned for the opening. Otherwise, the police of the city would be spread thin at all the separate parades occurring. The presence of the riot police in full gear so quickly meant someone on the inside had been working with them. Who that was Sebastian did not know.

His chest tightened. He pressed himself into the recess of a door and watched police run past the intersecting street. His breath came in short, ragged pants like that of a dog. He held out his hand and examining his fingers, found them shaking.

The chaos in the square and surrounding streets spread. The turn of events was unpredictable. He had no idea the city would ignite so easily. The energy coursing through the streets made him tremble every time shouts and footfalls drew near. What had he done? He suspected in the days between the park and festival he had become something more than a visitor to the city's ails. He feared he had become a conspirator who plotted to pull the strings of the city. The effect was frightening. Even more frightening was the thought that he had been the betrayer. He could, just as easily, have ferreted information to Grey. His actions had not been his own lately. The repeated lost time disturbed him. Something could have slipped in his search for the key to this changing city. He hoped that he remained true to his ethics and had not relented, as Xavi did.

"In here," a voice called out to him.

The old man from the squatters' underground station held a door open with one outstretched arm. Sebastian followed him through the door and up the stairs. He saw riot police storming through the streets. The sound of their boots reverberated in the stairwell. The building smelled of mold. Bust from the joints irritated his breath. The floorboards buckled as he went up, small creaks echoing through the shaft of the stairwell.

They had ascended several stories in the derelict building. Sebastian stopped the old man. "Where are you taking me now?"

"Come and see."

They emerged onto a rooftop at the top of the stairwell. Sebastian looked down the way they came and the prism of lines below looked like an infinite reflection as if an Escher drawing. On the roof, a garden grew. The plants were lush and flourished under the constant sunlight.

The old man pointed toward the city skyline. Sebastian had an unobstructed view from the edge. He saw the cathedrals, offices, tenements, parks, and the sea. It all blended together as one organism teeming with the life of its inhabitants. The city seemed more like a colony to Sebastian than some inorganic artifice depleted of life. The sun sparkled on the water. He watched protestors teeming through the streets. Blocks away, an old man played with his dog in the park. Young people rode bikes past him to grassy lawns where picnickers drank wine and ate.

The riot was spreading.

Someone upended a trash can and hurled it through the window of an electronics store. Looters stepped in and began robbing the place. Rioters pushed in unison, chanting "No More! No More!" A squad car rolled onto its side with the last push. The rioters ran under, pushing on the underbelly to upend the vehicle. People scattered out of the way as it toppled onto its sirens. The whirling lights crashed into the pavement as they shattered. One of the rioters climbed on top of the undercarriage and extended his arms in victory.

"What are you showing me?"

"There's no need to hide. It's all part of the same body. The differing parts coexist. Once you see it, you'll understand."

Riot police emerged onto the roof.

Rodrigo was thrown over the edge of the rooftop. He cursed at the security guards as he fell. Glass shattered. Storefront windows were broken. Designer clothes and electronics were looted. Citizens too poor to purchase the live broadcast in the media, congregated, spoke out, acted out their frustration on a city that drove them into the ground. Sebastian had a bracelet tightened around his wrists. Pepper sprayed his face. They carried him with their hands hooked under his elbows. The sounds of the riot came to him as he was led down the stairs back to the melee he had hatched. His legs stumbled down the steps he could not see.

They took him to a black sedan parked at the edge of the melee. The window rolled down. Grey looked at Sebastian, held up by the security guards.

"If someone is wronged, the punishment should equal the crime. This was not an equal response, wouldn't you say Sebastian?"

Sebastian spat on the ground.

"I've done nothing to deserve this kind of treatment. I can't have you harassing the peaceful work I do in this city."

"Why me? Why did you put me through all this?"

"Your story is no more important than any of the others in this city. There's nothing unique about you. Don't you get it now? There's tens of thousands of people just like you. Add those up and you get a pretty sum. That's what important. You're all nameless, faceless entries on a spreadsheet. Sums to be tallied."

"I don't believe you. You've spent too much effort on me, on it to be insignificant."

"There's hundreds, maybe thousands like me, all with enough clients like you to keep us occupied. There's even scripts to help us through. That's how routine this is for me. Let him go after I've gone. He's got nothing left for us."

"What about the site? This whole thing is about it. Does it even exist?"

"Exist? Of course it does. This will be the last thing I do for you. In the morning, when all of this is done, take him here." Grey placed a note in one of the guard's hands. The window rolled up and the car left.

*

Throughout the night, Sebastian saw sparks sprayed from handheld fireworks and smoke billowing from canisters of tear gas. The gold sparks showered the streets and the sides of buildings in a splattering of explosions. The two mixed in the night air leaving a sulfurous smell clinging to the back of his throat. Under the lampposts and sparks, the night took on an amber color. Shadows returned as the sparks passed. By the police barricades, bright halogen lights illuminated the expanse. It looked as bright as day where they were stationed. Patrols wore headlamps that banished the darkness from their path. Their circuits spread wider and wider, closer to the festivities on the Promenade. Sebastian heard intermittently the sound of conga drums played in parades and police shouting at rioters in the Old Quarter. The concordant sounds caused him pause. He tilted his head trying to mesh the two. He wondered whether the two would collide — the parade on the Promenade, lined with flower stalls and fireworks, and the riots coursing through the warren of the Old Quarter.

Fleeing executives, their ties askance, cowered behind tinted windows in luxury sedans and SUVs. They bought and sold officials in the city. The riot police moved like chess pieces pressing an advancing line. The wealthy and populists clashed like the waves of a storm, one that had been menacing the skyline for months, the torrent of which was wrenching the city. The downtrodden underclass, the missing family members were a caste of consumers meant to funnel all their worth upwards into a system that destroyed their heritage.

Halfway through the night, the security forces ran out of space. They undid the bracelets on Sebastian's wrists and pushed him into a car that took off away from the fracas. "Grey said we didn't have to keep you. You're lucky."

Did they participate willingly? Some did, too tired to resist. Others had small apartments and decades of secure work ahead. Sebastian knew nothing of that. He lived on the razor's edge, attempting to be free in all the chaos.

The car bounced roughly over the cobbled stone underneath. Sebastian rode on the cushioned backseat, melancholic over the loss of so much fervor. He had really believed that he could accomplish something. His prospects dissipated into the night, along with everything else in his life. Only a soft glow remained, like the neon he saw shimmering on water moments after the signs turned off. A small event horizon remained, through which he could not penetrate, only the faintest clue that anything had transpired.

"He's right, you know."

The escort beside him had spoken. He looked off abstractly at the passing city, nothing catching his interest for more than a moment.

"I see dozens like you. Every week we've got new charges to escort through the city. He treats all of them like this."

"I don't want to know."

"We never see them more than a few times. After that they're through. Nothing left. Sometimes I think I see them on the street, but they don't recognize me. I look like everyone else to them. Nothing unique about what I do either, I guess."

The four of them rode silently, watching the city pass. The streets blended together as they sped along, no one building distinguishing itself from the others crowding in.

"It's kind of sad, seeing so many people pass through without one recognizing you. You'd think people would pay more attention."

Sebastian couldn't take it anymore. He wanted to be free from mediocrity. Even though he had striven for anonymity for most of his life, now he found the emptiness suffocating. "Give me the address."

"You want it? Here. Doesn't matter much to us."

He took the address from his escorts and jumped out of the car. They yelled after him with instructions but he moved frantically, searching for the site. He quickly lost himself in the streets. The car must have skirted around, peering into the openings of side streets in search of him.

*

Gardenias dangled from iron lattice balconies. Red petals flowered for the night sky and green leaves crept down towards where he walked. The scent of the sea filled him as it wandered over cobbled stones, through corridors created between buildings, whose foundations were laid long before he could remember. The stones shifted with the shifting of earth to create rambling, curved paths. He looked at his fellow pedestrians and wondered how they could live among all this beauty and never stop to really see it. They carried themselves with such an unhurried air, as if they had seen a flower from every angle, in every light. He tried to explain this to them on a rooftop at the end of the night, but as he spoke he was amazed at how his speech was already gone, the moment it was spoken. Vowels and dipthongs danced about as notes strung loosely about the air. He listened to each vibration knowing that its beat had already ceased. From that point on, the evaporation of his speech into air and ears was an amusement all night. He spoke and was amazed by each and every sound.

I'm so tired, he thought. Just let it all go. Let everything go. No one wants to be moored in the past.

Everything had changed. His path was set, but he was never less sure of the streets through which he moved. The street emptied into a plaza. The plaza was lined with restaurants and clubs nestled under a colonnade. It was full with life in the early afternoon. In its center was a fountain where idlers passed the time under arching stone flourishes that trickled with cool waters.

Sebastian walked past the teenagers smoking in the plaza and looked into one of the passageways leading to where he stood. It was a small, cobbled street that appeared to lead off to nowhere in particular. He doubted that this angled path through squat white buildings would lead to a site of grand proportions. He tried another of the entranceways to the square and met the same. Another and another appeared to him as he paced along all sides of the plaza. The place had become a labyrinth to him. He decided he should retrace his steps. A new perspective would help him find his way, yet as he stepped from the threshold of the plaza, he found his footing unsure. The path he had chosen seemed no different to him than the ones he had observed before. His mind was uncertain of which entrance he had come from. Sebastian surely had known this area well at one point. Now his steps were faltering.

He remembered he had the building's address folded in his pocket. He retrieved the paper, unfolded it gingerly, and stared. He tilted his head first to one side then the other. Next he shuffled his hands around the paper, as he rotated it like a wheel. The revolutions revealed nothing of the loops and squiggles on the page.

The sudden idea came to him that he might be able to find the place by sight. He walked from one entrance of the square to another, rebounding from each entrance with equal confusion. He had crossed it several times before he evaluated the landscape surrounding him.

He looked at a white sign with black scribbling raised on its surface. One symbol looked like a line with a hook attached. Another, a pyramid on stilts. Sebastian stared at the symbols quizzically trying to understand why someone would create such a thing. He looked further down the street and saw that the signs were at every corner. They appeared in pairs, often pointing in perpendicular directions. Not being able to distinguish one from another, Sebastian followed one of the signs pointing down a crowded street. All the people's faces looked amused and sated. He could not help but be drawn to them.

Sebastian stood, feebly trying to retrace his steps, but in vain. His memory had failed. The city surrounding him was strange and foreign. He had no idea where to go or even where he stood at the moment. Even if Sebastian did remember the first street, there would be another, and another after that which he must traverse to get to his final destination.

A man stopped and asked if Sebastian was alright. Sebastian reeled. He felt his senses leaving him. Everything was not as he remembered. Even the signs he knew he should read were indecipherable to him. Without frame or reference, his faculties failed. He fell to the ground. The man who had inquired after him had already left, his business too important to inquire after another for long. Sebastian's head knocked against the stones in the square.

He lay there for some time as the sun passed overhead. They day grew hot. Flies peppered the air. To all who passed, he looked no more than a bum huddled next to the fountain. Other bums were lined around its base. The breeze from the water cooled their skin as they slept on beds of cardboard mats. The only difference was that the layer of grime under Sebastian's nails was less noticeable than the others.

*

The first sensation that Sebastian experienced was being pulled to his feet by two large black forms. Their frames were silhouetted by the sun. He could not make out their faces or clothing. "We've been looking for you."

"You can't stray like that. Something could happen."

Sebastian cringed as he leaned back against the curb of the fountain. His bones ached. The stones of the square had been an unkind place for rest. A wincing pain shot through his head. Sebastian remembered the dread of not having any anchor, any reference. The terror made sweat condense on his spine. It chilled him to think of such a feeling of loss. He quickly directed his thoughts back to the world around him. The two black forms hovered above him, blocking out the sting of the afternoon light. The scene bustled around him in the afternoon. People strode. Others ambled. The scent of coffee and falafel wafted in the air. These were definable, knowable sensations that Sebastian felt grateful to rely upon. The sense of terror left him. His gaze stayed focused outward.

"You should really be more careful when listening to directions."

"Our directions were explicit. We drove around to the site. It's always much quicker to drive there."

"You were so determined to walk that we didn't have the heart to stop you."

Sebastian lifted himself up off the curb. A rush of blood entered his head. His joints still ached a little, but he was more than capable of maneuvering by himself. He

197

recognized the two as his escort's from Grey's earlier. "Where am I?" he stammered.

"This is the square we told you about. The building site is right over there." The first pointed over Sebastian's shoulder with a fat, calloused finger.

Sebastian spun. Before him was the fountain. It spurted streams over water over his view of a mammoth construction site. All guts and bones at the moment, it seemed more cloud of activity than anything tangible. Workman clambered over girders. The sound of rivets plummeted into Sebastian's ears. A haze of dust blew about them as they worked, perhaps from the cement being mixed or the ground being exhumed. Sebastian recognized each individual facet as what should be considered construction but it all seemed in disarray. Their actions had no order. It seemed as a workman carried materials up the elevator, another was breaking them down, tossing them from above. The waste would accumulate in large explosions of dust and noise at the base of the structure. Some gathered the materials and ground them up to make more, which were once again hauled up and dismantled.

"You wanted to see it, didn't you?"

And in those final moments, Sebastian, too, disappeared.

ABOUT WHITNEY POOLE

Whitney Poole has lived in Baltimore, Barcelona, Glasgow, New York, Osaka and Seattle. He earned his MFA in Creative Writing from George Mason University and his MA in Writing from Johns Hopkins University.

39821754R00117

Made in the USA
Lexington, KY
12 March 2015